The President's Daughter

(A Donovan Creed Novel - Volume 13)

John Locke

THE PRESIDENT'S DAUGHTER

Cover Designed by: Claudia Jackson
Copyright © shutterstock 955843336
Copyright © shutterstock 777962374

Published by John Locke Books, LLC

Visit the author's websites:
http://www.daniripper.com
http://www.donovancreed.com

ISBN 978-1-937656-17-1 (eBook)
ISBN 978-1-937656-18-8 (Paperback)

Version 2017.12.28

Medical Warning:

Talk to your doctor before beginning a John Locke series, as studies have shown them to be habit-forming and highly addictive. Do not read Locke if you suffer from high blood pressure or other heart-related issues, as readers often experience mood swings, increased pulses, elevated heart rates, and have reported unexpected shifts in body position that take them to the edge of their seats. Do not drive or use machinery while reading Locke novels.

Locke novels are not for everyone, and may cause serious reactions including insomnia, night terrors, and uncontrollable, maniacal laughter. Tell your doctor right away if you have these, or if you experience unusual changes in your behavior including increased sexual urges, palpitations, or prolonged erections. Common side effects include confusion, hysteria, and trouble swallowing a given premise.

Do not drink alcohol while reading Locke novels, though those with a history of drug or alcohol abuse may be more prone to understanding the material. Adverse reactions to Locke novels include nausea and vomiting, loss of appetite, severe itching, rectal bleeding, purple spots under the skin, and Jimmy Legs. In extreme cases, readers have reported laughing so hard they not only shit their pants, but other's pants, as well. Upon completing a Locke series be prepared to experience symptoms of withdrawal, including fear, anger, extreme sadness, and moderate to severe depression.

Ask your doctor today if John Locke novels are right for you!

John Locke

New York Times Best Selling Author

Has received more than 10,000 Five-Star Reviews!

8th Member of the Kindle Million Sales Club

(Members include James Patterson, George R.R. Martin, and Lee Child)

John Locke had 4 of the top 10 eBooks on Amazon/Kindle at the same time, including #1 and #2!

...Had 6 of the top 20 books at the same time!

...Had 8 books in the top 43 at the same time!

...Has written 36 books in seven years in six separate genres,

All best-sellers!

...Has been published throughout the world in numerous languages by the world's most prestigious publishing houses!

...Winner, Second Act Magazine's Story of the Year!

...Named by Time Magazine as one of the "Stars of the DIY-Publishing Era"

Wall Street Journal: "John Locke (is) transforming the 'book' business"

Donovan Creed Series:

Lethal People
Lethal Experiment
Saving Rachel
Now & Then
Wish List
A Girl Like You
Vegas Moon
The Love You Crave
Maybe
Callie's Last Dance
Because We Can!
This Means War!
The President's Daughter

Emmett Love Series:

Follow the Stone
Don't Poke the Bear
Emmett & Gentry
Goodbye, Enorma
Rag Soup
Spider Rain

Dani Ripper Series:

Call Me!
Promise You Won't Tell?
Teacher, Teacher
Don't Tell Presley!
Abbey Rayne
Hot Mess Express!

Dr. Gideon Box Series:

Bad Doctor
Box
Outside the Box
Boxed In!

Other:

Kill Jill
Casting Call
When David Died
Sorority Girl
Daisy & Bobby

Kindle Worlds:

A Kiss for Luck (Kindle Only)

Non-Fiction:

How I sold 1 Million eBooks in 5 Months!

Author's Comment:

Those who say, "God never gives you more than you can handle" have never met Donovan Creed or Callie Carpenter.

The President's Daughter

1

INTRODUCTION

IF NOT FOR the old photo of Darrell pretending to fuck a goat, my wife Trudy might have escaped.

She and I had fallen asleep in the master bedroom of a Denver condo I rented for the weekend. Around 2:00 a.m. I woke to the slight, sudden sound a photograph makes when it falls to the floor.

It wasn't loud, but I'm a light sleeper and any unexpected noise gets my attention.

I sat up, reached for Trudy, realized she wasn't in the bed. Relaxing slightly, I called her name, then my upper chest exploded. As I rolled off the bed, away from the shooter, I chided myself for making that involuntary noise everyone makes when they take a bullet they weren't expecting. It's like you're shouting "*Hee!*" and "*Uhh!*" at the same time. Thankfully, Callie Carpenter wasn't there, or I never would have lived it down. I knew—even in the moment—that for the rest of her life, Callie would greet me by making that sound. And

I would've deserved it because...this is what happens when you're on vacation with your wife, and you let your guard down. You make rookie mistakes.

But I hadn't been a complete rookie.

As I rolled off the bed I grabbed the flashlight I'd placed on Trudy's nightstand hours earlier. Significant, because anything in the palm of my hand is a weapon: a toothpick. A napkin. A paper clip. A gummy bear. The flashlight wasn't big, but it was aluminum alloy, military grade; uncommonly bright.

I knew I had to remain silent. In the old days, all alone as a sniper in the military, that was a lot easier. Back then when you got shot, you'd lie quietly till the enemy gave you a better target. Then you'd shoot him. But I'm older now, mid-forties, and I'm not the same man I was in my early twenties.

I'm better.

More experienced.

More patient.

To keep things in perspective, everything I told you so far about the condo shooting occurred within a split second. I moved so quickly, by the time Trudy's voice could be heard from the bathroom I was already on the floor. But the words she spoke weren't the ones I expected. I thought she'd scream: "*Donovan*! Are you *okay*?" But what she yelled was, "You *shot* him?"

And her cousin Abner said, "I had to. You woke his ass up."

As the light came on in the bathroom, Abner saved my life by hollering, "Turn that off! I'm wearin' night vision goggles."

"Sorry."

By then Trudy was in the bedroom. "Is he dead?"

"I ain't sure. But he's definitely dyin'."

"Damn it, Abner! I *love* him! I just wanted to leave. I didn't want him to *die*!"

"Well, you shouldn't have woke him. What do you want me to do?"

Trudy called my name, but I kept still. She sighed deeply and said, "I guess you'd better shoot him again, just to be safe. Otherwise, he'll kill us both. Do it quick, I'll be in the car."

The revelation that Abner was wearing light-enhancement equipment was huge, since I knew it would only require 85 lumens of light to disorient, and temporarily blind him. If I were relying on a standard household flashlight, I'd have been screwed, since those devices typically produce a mere 10 to 60 lumens. But I use tactical military flashlights, and the one in my hand could generate 3,800 lumens, which meant I could literally...

Wait.

You see where this is going. No need to dwell on the magnitude of the mismatch. The short version is, from the moment I grabbed the flashlight, Abner's life expectancy dropped to thirty seconds, max. Indeed, I killed him so quickly my dear, sweet Trudy didn't have time to exit the condo. When I tackled her, she stayed down, but I scrambled to my feet in time to kick the knife from her hand.

"I was plannin' to leave quietly," she said, "but Abner wanted that damned picture of Darrell with the goat, from back when they were kids. I was fetchin' it from my suitcase."

"Why, Trudy?"

"Who knows? It's the dumbest picture ever. But that's Abner for you."

"I meant, why were you leaving me?"

"Are you serious? You just murdered my cousin!"

"He *shot* me."

"Oh, please. You would've eventually killed him. You already killed half my kinfolk."

"That's not remotely true. You've got a thousand relatives, and I've killed exactly four."

"So far as you know."

"Trudy—"

"Donovan? Lord knows I love you, and I'm grateful you saved my life back when all that bad stuff went down, but ever since we got married you've made me a prisoner in my own home."

"Trudy, I've *been* in prison. *Several* prisons, in fact, in three different countries. And I *promise* you, living in our hundred-million-dollar estate is a better experience."

"Maybe so, but we're locked away in the middle of nowhere, always worried someone's gonna kill us. Remember the fruit basket incident? No one should have to live like that. You're gone half the time, and no one ever visits. I used to have Hawley, but you sent her off to live with a witch."

"I did that for *your* protection. Like you told me a thousand times, Hawley's a handful."

"A *handful*? She threatened to blow my head off my shoulders!"

"All the more reason to let Rose teach her how to control her temper."

"And her witchy powers."

"The point is, Hawley's dangerous, and I had to protect you. I'm sorry you miss her. I do, too. She's *my* daughter, after all."

"Hawley's just one seed in the turd, Donovan. I weren't meant to be sheltered. I grew up among lots of family and friends."

"Your family and friends were killers, thieves, and meth heads."

"Not all of 'em. Back in Kentucky I had some decent, normal friends. But *who's* allowed to visit me? *No* one."

"What about Callie?"

"*Fruit basket* Callie? She's *your* friend, not mine. You used to *date* her. And I think you'll agree I'm being charitable to put it that way."

"You are. Thank you."

"And she's not your friend, in any case."

"You can't possibly mean that. Callie's the best friend I've ever had."

"That's plain pitiful, Donovan, seein' as how you won't even let her on the property without a full body scan for weapons."

"That's just me, being cautious. She's a trained killer. A professional assassin."

Trudy sighed. "That's the point I'm tryin' to make. The woman you consider the best friend you ever had poisoned you once, just to see if the *antidote* would work. And don't think I forgot how she murdered your ex-girlfriend in a jealous rage, then came back after the funeral and threw herself on the grave and stabbed the dirt with a butcher's knife."

"Look: I'll admit Callie's got issues, if you'll admit she wouldn't hesitate to put her life on the line to protect you."

"Of *course*, she will. Until you tell her to kill me."

"Forget Callie," I said. "This whole prison thing is ridiculous. You live like a queen."

Trudy sighed. "That part's true. I s'pect we live better than anyone in the world. I mean, the way you've provided for me is *crazy* good. But it's your version of what a woman ought to want, not mine. You know I'd be happier in a three-bedroom ranch in a nice, normal neighborhood, with a little garden I could tend, and girlfriends who'd come over for coffee."

"That sounds fun for a day or two, but after that, what's there to talk about?"

"Why, lots of things! We'd share recipes and gossip and make fun of our neighbors and complain about our shiftless husbands and lazy kids, and stuff like that. And you and me would have so much more fun goin' to restaurants and movies and dancin'. And on the weekends, we'd have the neighbors over for barbecue, and–"

"I get it!" I said. "You're right: sounds like hell on earth."

"To you, maybe."

I took a deep breath. "You didn't have to say yes when I proposed. You could have stayed married to your brother."

"For the millionth time, he weren't my brother, he was my cousin."

"Yeah, but you didn't know that at the time."

"You're changin' the subject of how we never go anywhere together, or do anything fun."

"We're in Denver right *now*!" I said. "On *vacation*."

"Right, and how's *that* goin' for you?"

"Honestly? I've had better."

"Me too." She paused. "Where'd he shoot you?"

"Chest."

"How bad are you hurt?"

"I'm not sure yet."

"Well, you'd best get it looked at."

"Thanks for your concern," I say, dryly. "I'll be sure to do that."

"My pleasure. What happens now?"

"*You* know what happens."

"You're gonna *kill* me?" She paused. "Is it because you're pissed or because I know too much?"

"Neither. It's because you wouldn't last twenty-four hours in the real world without my protection. My enemies will hunt you down and kill you an inch at a time."

"I don't know about that. I'm pretty resourceful."

"Like you said, remember the fruit basket incident? You wouldn't stand a chance. And I love you too much to let you suffer."

Trudy said, "Here's an idea: what if I tried real hard to be happy again? If you could find it in your heart to spare me, maybe we can get back to the way we were when we first got married."

"That's tempting, since I retain a vague memory of what it was like to have sex. But I'm not sure I could get past how casually you told Abner to shoot me a second time, 'just to be safe,' while you waited in the car."

"You heard that, huh?"

"Yup."

"Is there anything I can say or do to keep you from killing me?"

"Nothing comes to mind."

"What about a blow job?"

"I've been shot, remember?"

She paused. "Will you do me *one* favor?"

"Name it."

"Tell Hawley I never stopped lovin' her."

"She knows that. You saved her life."

"Like you said, Hawley ain't an easy child to raise, and not bein' her natural birth mother, I'd understand if people say I couldn't have loved her as much as her sleazy hooker mom did."

"They won't say that in front of me."

"Thank you, Donovan. I always loved *you*, too."

"I know."

"It's just...you have this way of puttin' people in constant danger and suckin' the life out of 'em."

"So I've been told."

"Miss me, okay?"

"I will."

"You promise?"

"Always."

That was three months ago. And I *have* missed her.

Every damn day.

II

THE FRUIT BASKET INCIDENT

ONE OF THE toughest things about marriage, every day there's a test. And the way you handle that test will determine whether you strengthened your relationship that day, or weakened it. In fairness to Trudy, I'm sure I failed 90% of those daily tests, and the "fruit basket incident" was only the last straw. The way it went down, about six months before Abner shot me in the chest, I was out of town, doing what hitmen do. After whacking Marty "The Duck" Spinelli, I called Trudy to check on her. The conversation started out great, but took a bad turn when she innocently said, "By the way, next time you see Callie, be sure to thank her for the fruit basket. It's gorgeous!"

It took a split-second to register, then I freaked out and started yelling. I couldn't believe my security team would allow a fruit basket in our house. Trudy tried to calm me down by repeating that Callie sent it.

"I don't give a shit *who* sent it! Are there bananas?"

"Yes, of course," Trudy said. "And they're beautiful."

"Where's the basket right now?"

"What do you mean?"

"Where's the fucking basket?"

"On the kitchen counter. And I don't appreciate your tone."

"Did you or Hawley touch it?"

"No. Well, I mean, if we're being technical, I read the card."

"*Shit!*"

"Donovan?" she said. "Relax. It's a fruit basket, not a bomb."

I shouted: "Take all your clothes off, put them in a plastic trash bag, and tie it as tight as you can. Then put that bag in another one, and double-tie it. Then take a hot shower and scrub every inch of your body. Meanwhile, I'll call Anson and have him isolate the area!"

Trudy took a deep breath before saying, "I know you're stressed about whatever it is you've been doing the past few days. But you need to chill, Donovan, because this is insane."

"Trudy, *listen* to me!"

She said, "I'm gonna say this one last time, and then I'm hanging up: I've seen more than my share of fruit baskets, and that's all this is."

"Are you *kidding* me?" I shouted. "Do you have any idea how many people I've killed with fruit baskets?"

"Stop it, Donovan. You're either kidding, or crazy. Either way, I'm hanging up."

"Trudy, don't be stupid! Someone brings a fruit basket into MY house? It could be infested with spider eggs."

"*What?*"

"Brazilian Wandering Spiders. After your shower, grab Hawley and get out of the house, and don't go near anyone who touched the basket. We might have to burn the whole fucking house down."

Trudy sighed. "Fine. I'll do everything you said, because I want you to calm down. And when you get home you can decide between seeing a therapist, or getting a divorce. Because I'm not gonna live like this much longer."

True to her word, she didn't.

Now that she's gone, I'll concede the point that I'm not an easy man to live with. And I'll also state for the record that I will never fall in love, ever again. You have my word.

III

I SHOULD POINT OUT...

I DIDN'T KILL Trudy that night, nor have I killed her since. Instead, I called in some favors, got her into protective custody, obtained a quickie divorce, and got the US Marshalls' office to put her in Witness Protection, so she could start a new life. I also legally changed my daughter's name from Hawley Creed to Hawley Stout, and named my witchy friend Rose as her legal guardian.

"What about money?" Trudy asked on our last day together.

"What do you think is fair?"

"A thousand a month?"

"*What?*"

"Just till I get my feet on the ground. I plan to waitress, so I s'pect wherever they put me I'll get a decent job pretty quick."

"I can't pay you by the month, Trudy. You need to understand how this works: we can't see or talk to each other, ever again. You'll have a different name. What I'm saying, I'll have to pay you a lump sum."

"In that case, can you spare $12,000?"

"I can spare twenty million."

She smiled. "Even better."

As we kissed goodbye the enormity of the situation hit me: the woman I loved with all my heart was going to eventually live the rest of her life with someone else, and I'll never know how things turned out for her. I'll never know if she married, had kids of her own, or if her husband ever mistreats her. I won't know when she's sick, hurt, happy, or sad. If she winds up in the hospital, dying a slow death from a terrible disease, I'll never know, and won't be there to comfort her.

In the lonely hours, days, and weeks that followed our breakup, I became overwhelmed by the total emptiness of my enormous home. Depressed, I focused on all the quirky things I missed about Trudy that made her such an original. Sure, we made love and went places and did all the things other couples do in the early years of their relationships. But it was her devastating *absence* that taught me true love doesn't occur on a trip, in a bedroom, or at a special event. It's hidden between the conscious moments of our lives.

I was surprised and slightly hurt by the strength she showed that day when she ended our kiss. "Take care of yourself," she said.

"You too."

She grinned. "You chose this moment to mention an Irish band? Weird!"

With that, she laughed, tossed her hair, and left the room, taking all the oxygen with her.

Interesting side note: when I called my banker in Zurich to tell him where to wire Trudy's twenty million he informed me my account had a zero balance. I'll spare you the details of our tense conversation, but suffice it to say I was unhappy to learn my Swiss bank account wasn't as un-hackable as I'd been led to believe.

How much did I lose?

One billion dollars.

Yes, I still had thirty million in a USA account, but after wiring Trudy's twenty million, I was down to my last ten million. I know that sounds like a lot, but the upkeep on my house, staff, security, and expenses runs eight million a year. So, I was forced to let everyone go except Anson, two guards, a maintenance man, and two groundskeepers. As bad as things were, I refused to put my house up for sale, believing I could either recover the stolen money or earn enough to continue living my insane lifestyle.

After paying everyone a fair severance and bringing all my bills current, I was down to $1,505,608. Before you tell me how well you could live on that sum of money, let me remind you the annual taxes on my estate are $1.5 million. And they were due in six weeks.

To put it bluntly, for the first time in my adult life, I was broke.

I know what you're thinking: what about all the money I make working for Sensory Resources?

My job is secret, remember? They pay me nothing.

So, I've gone back to free-lance killing, mostly for the mob. Fifty grand here, a hundred grand there.

Not nearly enough.

So whenever feasible, I supplement by stealing from the people I kill.

Which brings us to the present.

PART 1

Donovan Creed

Chapter 1

WANT TO KNOW how to kill a married guy?

Find out what he's hiding from his wife, and use it against him.

I'm not talking about "killing him" in the sense of hurting his relationship. I'm literally referring to taking a man's life.

By way of example, Rocco's wife Jessica thinks he's having an affair because he recently started taking care of his body. He's working out, watching what he eats, and rises early for his twice-a-day run.

Run?

There's the key.

Running is defined as a pace faster than eight minutes per mile, so I guarantee you this fat bastard isn't running. What I'm saying, Rocco's just started this fitness thing, so there's no way he's *running* at all, much less twice-a-day. At best, he's jogging.

But he's not doing it because he's having an affair.

I mean, yeah, he's having an affair, but that's not why he's running twice-a-day. His affair's been going on for years, but his girlfriend, Ursula, doesn't give a shit about the size of his belly. She's just trying to get through life as a single mom on a cashier's pay, so she gives

Rocco the "girlfriend experience" he craves and he gives her enough cash to pay the bills and fund a modest lifestyle.

Don't get me wrong, Rocco loves Jessica and the kids and would give up anything in the world for them—except two things. But Jessica being Jessica, those are the only ones she's asked him to quit: smoking and the mob.

Rocco can't quit smoking because it's a lifelong addiction, but he promised Jessica he would, so instead of smoking, he runs twice a day. As for the mob, he contacted the U.S. Marshall's office, offering to exchange damaging testimony for Witness Protection, which is how I got involved in this domestic drama. When Sal Bonadello (an organized crime boss) got tipped off about Rocco's plans, he hired me to "Kill the rat bastard!"

So here I am, on foot, following Rocco from a distance. Ten minutes of surveillance makes it clear his hour-long "jog" only carries him a quarter mile in each direction. Four blocks from his home, near the corner of Blackstrap and Molasses, he keeps several packs of cigarettes hidden under the bottom of a mailbox, using Velcro to hold them in place. He grabs a pack, smokes it while walking at a very slow pace, then gargles with the travel-size bottle of mouthwash he keeps in the pocket of his running shorts, spits it out, and jogs back home to tell the wife how well he's maintaining his running regime.

At least I assume that's what he tells her.

After following him home, I return to the mailbox, remove the three remaining packs of cigarettes, and take them to my car. If the packs had been open it would have taken less than two minutes to lace each cigarette with poison. But unfortunately, the packs are sealed, which makes it a nightmare. Poisoning the cigarettes from a single pack in a manner that makes the box appear to be factory-sealed takes two hours and requires a scalpel, syringe, a vial of deadly poison*, a hand-held steamer, and a glue gun. And no, I didn't have the steamer and glue gun in my kit, so I had to go buy them.

Now, after all that effort, I look at the other two packs and decide, "Fuck it." I'll let Rocco assume someone found his stash and was nice enough to leave him a single pack.

---

*You may be wondering what type of poison I placed in Rocco's cigarettes. The truth is, I don't know, since I only ask my scientists two things: "What's the best poison for my intended use, and how do I keep from killing myself when handling it?" That said, I *do* know that this particular combination of elements includes cone snail venom, which contains more than 50 different chemicals that target the brain and nervous system. I heard one of the guys say it's 1,000 times stronger than morphine!

Suffice it to say, when Rocco "jogs" to the mailbox later today, it'll be a one-way trip.

Chapter 2

AFTER PARKING MY rental car near the mailbox all afternoon to make sure the right guy dies, I finally spot Rocco lumbering down the road. When he gets to the corner he reaches under the mailbox, frowns, then gets on his hands and knees and looks underneath it. He grabs the tainted pack, swears, looks up and down the street as if he thinks he'll be able to tell who stole the two missing packs. He stands, kicks the mailbox, then grabs the back of his thigh and curses again, apparently having pulled his hamstring. As he opens the deadly pack, my phone pings with the text message: *Experto Crede*, which tells me General Hank Barry's trying to reach me. Barry being the former head of Homeland Security and current White House Chief of Staff.

Experto Crede is his safe word, his signature. It's a Latin phrase that connotes trust, as in: *trust the expert*. All my closest contacts have a signature word or phrase that identifies them. Callie Carpenter's is *Amaranthus*, a flower also known as *Love Lies Bleeding*. Leave it to Callie, right? At any rate, when these signature words come to me via text it lets me know they're going to call me on a burner phone to discuss urgent private business. Sal's word is *Cannoli*. Anson's is–well, it's not important. And anyway, my phone's ringing.

When I answer, General Barry says, "Hi Donovan. How's the wife?"

"Which one?"

"Who gives a shit? I'm trying to make small talk."

I laugh. "You had a wonderful, distinguished career, and *now* look at you. What were you *thinking*?"

"Someone had to step up and save the world."

I'd love to give him some shit about his job, his boss, and the world in general, but I'm too busy watching Rocco light his cigarette. "What can I do for you, General?"

Instead of answering, he asks, "What's the most you ever made for a single job?"

"Two million."

"How'd you like to make four?"

My eyes go wide. He wants me to kill the president.

He laughs. "It's not who you think."

"When can we meet?"

"I can't. It's too sensitive. My job is to secure the asset. Are you on board?"

"Of course. Who's the target?"

"You'll find everything you need in the packet."

I watch Rocco's body crumple to the ground. He's foaming at the mouth, trying to call for help, but his voice is inaudible.

"Where's the packet?"

General Barry says, "Not so fast, Donovan. The buyers need reassurance."

"What do you mean?"

"They're newbies. Nervous. They want to see how you handle a medium-profile target before giving you the job."

"They want an *audition*?"

"Yes."

"How much for that one?"

"It's on you."

"What do you mean?"

"They want you to do it for free."

"So, you lied about the four million?"

"Not at all."

"You asked what's the most I ever made for a single job, then offered me $4 million for the second job. But it's *two* jobs for four million. *If* they decide to give me the second job."

"Actually, the second job pays $8 million. That's why I said four. I did the math for you, in advance."

"Eight million for a single hit."

"That's correct."

"And it's not the president?"

"No. Any other questions?"

"Yeah. Who's the unlucky bastard they chose for the audition?"

"Chuck Boyle."

"You say that like I'm supposed to know him."

"He's an investigative reporter for the Beltway Daily News Observer."

The last few seconds of Rocco's life are touching. The way he's trying to drag himself home puts me in mind of how dying elephants always start walking toward "the elephant graveyard." Except that whole thing about the elephants is a myth, because—Tarzan movies notwithstanding—elephants die where they die. Likewise, Rocco expires a mere ten feet from the mailbox. I put my car in gear and ask, "Any special instructions for the Boyle hit?"

"Nope."

He gives me Chuck's home and business addresses, the make and model of his car, and a couple of phone numbers.

"Tell me about his family."

"Why?"

"It's my job."

"He's married. Two or three kids, I think."

"What's the wife's name?"

"How the fuck should I know?"

"Does she work?"

"No clue."

"How old are the kids?"

He pauses. "Are you *shitting* me? What the fuck's going on? You never asked me these types of questions before."

"I never worked for free before."

"I gave you everything I've got. Get her done, Son."

Chapter 3

CHUCK BOYLE'S A busy man.

It took twenty hours to get him on the phone and when I finally did he asked more questions than Alex Trebek on meth. But I refused to tell him my name, my position with Homeland Security, and what type of damaging insider information I was pretending to have on the White House Administration. When he pressed harder, I hung up and waited for him to call me back.

He waited too, but the fear of losing an exclusive weakened his resolve. When he called me back I told him I changed my mind. Yes, my information was huge, I lied, but I told him I could lose my job, and possibly my life, so... "I can't go through with it," I said. "Please lose my number." I hung up again, and that had the same effect as setting the hook when the bass hits the lure. Chuck called me back and gave me the hard-sell, and I reluctantly agreed to meet him in a public place of his choosing (but not too public) and told him to come alone. He gave me the name of a local watering hole and said he'd either be sitting at the bar or in a corner booth at 7:00 p.m. tonight, and that I could approach him at my convenience any time before eight.

Now, glancing at my phone, I can see that Chuck's been in the bar waiting for me for at least twenty minutes.

Am I running late?

Not at all. I'm in Chuck's townhouse, on Capitol Square Plaza, searching all his drawers and closets.

He comes home shortly after ten, pissed as hell. I hear him talking on the phone as he enters, so I hide in the kitchen pantry till he finishes the call. When I hear the refrigerator door open, I sneak up behind him and put him in a choke hold till he loses consciousness. Then I bind him to a chair with nylon cable ties, and gag him. When he comes to, I say, "Chuck, I don't know if you've ever been choked out before, but if not, you're about to experience the worst headache of your life." I point to a tablet and glass of water on the table beside him and add, "That pill will mitigate the pain, but I'll understand if you don't trust me enough to take it. Do you?"

He shakes his head, no.

"Very well. Just know it's there, in case you change your mind. In the meantime, I'm going to remove your gag. Feel free to scream, if you wish, but your neighbors won't be able to hear you, since I injected your vocal chords with a numbing agent. At most, you'll be able to whisper."

I remove his gag and wait for him to scream.

When he does, he realizes I was telling the truth.

Now, with wide, terrified eyes, he whispers, "Is this some sort of warning?"

"What do you mean?"

He whispers, "I wrote something that upset the president. I assume you're warning me to back off."

"Not really," I say. "In fact, no offense, but until two days ago I never even *heard* of you. But yesterday I spent hours reading your articles, and I'm sure you *did* upset the president. But this isn't a warning, Chuck."

"It's not?"

I shake my head.

"Then why are you here?"

"I've been hired to kill you."

"By *whom?*"

"Does it matter?"

As you'd expect, Chuck spends the next thirty seconds trying to break free, but what sort of hitman would I be if that were remotely possible? I wait till he tires himself out, and by then his head is ready to explode from the pain. I force feed him the pill and make him drink the entire glass of water, since hydration is as important as the medication when it comes to relieving headaches. I tell him: "Chuck, I personally think you're a brilliant writer, and I have the utmost respect for your work. But I've got a job to do, so..."

Chuck's instinct for self-preservation kicks in: "I'll stop writing inflammatory articles! I'll abandon my current project. I'll pay you to let me go. I'll quit my job entirely, sell my house, and move away." He offers to do anything I ask, and begs me to consider his wife and kids.

Not that anything he said makes a difference, but he *has* piqued my interest, so I ask, "Just for clarity, how much money *could* you pay?"

"A hundred and fifty-thousand dollars," he whispers, earnestly. "Give or take."

"And where are your wife and kids?"

"Connecticut. We're separated." He quickly adds, "But we're working things out. She's moving back soon."

"When?"

"Next month."

"You cheated on her?"

He nods.

Chuck's a hard-luck guy. The kind who could fall in a river of titties and come out sucking his thumb. I tell him: "Ruth and the kids aren't coming back, Chuck."

He looks at me. "What do you mean?"

"This townhouse is eighteen hundred square feet with a one-car garage. You purchased it four months ago for $960,000. Ruth and the kids never lived here and you're not expecting them to join you next month because you're divorced, not separated. As for your relationship with your kids, I couldn't help but notice how few photos you have. And they're in a box on the top shelf of your closet. This isn't a family's home, Chuck, it's a bachelor pad wannabe. Ruth is happily dating a guy named Alan Mercer, who owns a landscaping company in New Haven. Your kids are enrolled full-time in school. And you don't have a hundred and fifty thousand dollars to pay me."

"I do! I swear!"

"Stop lying, Chuck, I've done my homework. You have no savings account, less than five grand in checking, you're two months behind in your alimony and child-support, and you've exhausted your IRA. You wear mom jeans, troll bars, and your only source of income is your job, with a salary far less than I would've expected for a writer of your ability. In short, you're barely making ends meet. But I *am* interested in two things you said. Let's start with this: what did you mean when you said you'd do anything I want?"

"I-I'm not sure what you're asking."

"What was going through your mind when you made that offer?"

He says nothing.

"Your statement covers a lot of ground, Chuck. '*I'll do anything you want*,' you said. You must have had *something* in mind."

"I just meant, if there's anything you want, anything I can do for you, like a favor, or whatever, consider it done."

"You don't mean that."

"I *do*! I swear to *God*!"

I take a deep breath and let it out slowly. "You've peeled the scab off my pet peeve, Chuck. People always *say* that, but they never mean it."

"*I* mean it."

"You *think* you do, because at this very moment you'll say anything to survive. But life isn't like the *Oliver Twist* song. I won't be asking you to climb a hill or paint your face bright blue. If I let you live you'd owe me an Ultimate Favor. The type you can't refuse. And I guarantee that even now, with your life on the line, you're not prepared to grant me an Ultimate Favor."

"Test me."

"Very well. Let's say I wanted sex."

"I'd do it."

I laugh. "Not with *you*, Chuck. Your daughter."

"*What*? She's eight years *old*!"

"Relax, Chuck. I'm not interested in your daughter. I'm just pointing out that an Ultimate Favor is *not* something you want to owe. Forget the sex. How about I drive you to New Haven tonight and force you to murder your children with an axe?"

"You wouldn't ask that."

"You have no idea what I'd ask, and that's my point: you can't make an open-ended offer like that. You can't offer to do anything I ask. What if I needed you to blow up a school full of kids, or a newborn's nursery at your local hospital?"

He stares at me in horror, as if trying to comprehend how I could possibly consider these types of examples to be favors. Eventually he says, "I stand corrected."

I frown. "Sorry to make this all about me, Chuck. You're about to die, and here I am, giving you a lecture. I apologize."

As the reality of his impending death sinks in, the tears start flowing from his eyes. I ask him to tell me about the project he's currently working on, which was the second thing he said earlier that piqued my interest. He does, and we talk about it for a while. I ask a boatload of questions, and he tells me how to access the notes and documents on his computer. I tell him it's a helluva story and add,

"If I can, I'll make sure it gets published. And if it does, it'll be under your name."

Like Trudy did, he asks if there's anything he can say or do to prevent me from killing him tonight, and to prove there's not, I take his life immediately, as painlessly as possible. I'd planned to stage the scene as a drug overdose, but the rope burns on his wrists and ankles force me to set him on fire, instead. So, I dowse him with gasoline, but before lighting the match, I download the information from his computer, then take a moment to respect Chuck and his profession. Because it takes guts to be an investigative reporter in Washington. Because the bigger your target, the more powerful your enemies.

And Chuck hasn't just *criticized* the president, he *criminalized* him.

How bad was the story Chuck's been working on?

Really bad.

But it has nothing to do with the president. It's a full-fledged expose on General Barry.

Before leaving Chuck's townhouse I call the general. When he answers, I say, "It's done."

Barry tells me to get a room under my name at the Ritz-Carlton in Georgetown and wait for further instructions. When I fail to hang up immediately, he asks, "Was there anything else?"

I want to say, *"In fact, there IS something, General: you LIED to me! The person or people offering me eight million dollars didn't require proof of my ability. THEY didn't want Chuck Boyle dead, YOU did! He was about to destroy your career, so you got ME to kill him FOR you. Not only that, but you tricked me into doing it for free!"*

But I don't say that, because I don't want to tip my hand. If General Barry thought I knew about Chuck's story, or had his notes and documents, I'd never get the eight-million-dollar job. Worse, he'd have me fired from Sensory, throw me into a full-scale IRS audit, and hire a rude group of people to kill me. None of those things would achieve the intended result, but they'd certainly cause more grief than I care to endure.

So, I say nothing about Chuck's story. Not just because I need the eight million, but because General Barry knew I'd be willing to perform an audition hit for free.

Which means he knows I'm broke.

Which means he probably knows what happened to my Swiss bank account.

"There's nothing else," I say. "I'll be at the hotel in twenty minutes."

Chapter 4

AN HOUR PASSES before I hear the knock at the door, but I'm not in my hotel room, I'm in the room directly across the hall, so when I open the door it startles the beautiful thirty-something woman. I tell her I'm Donovan, and she introduces herself as Charlotte, and I give her a light hug before letting her enter the room I'm supposed to have.

"Thanks, Donovan," she says. "That was really sweet."

Glad she thinks so, but I was only checking to make sure she wasn't wearing a bomb.

After closing the door behind us, I ask her to remove her clothes. She gives me an odd look, as if I'm being a bit too eager, but again, my motive is safety. I'm checking for wires. As she undresses, I check through her purse. When I look up she strikes a pose with one hand over her head and the other on her hip and says, "Satisfied?"

I am. In fact, I can barely catch my breath. She's truly stunning. "Can you turn for me, please?"

When she does, I say, "Not to impose, but could you bend forward and spread your cheeks?"

She turns back to face me and shows me a frown. "Are you for *real?*"

"I like the view."

"Well, I'm sorry, Donovan, but *that* view's off the table."

I let it slide, since the odds are extremely low that she's concealed a weapon in such a small space. I tell her to please get dressed.

"You want me to put my clothes back on? All of them?"

"Yes."

When she's fully dressed I escort her across the hall and enter the second room I booked.

With mild trepidation, she asks, "Whose room is this?"

"Mine. I booked it under a different name."

"Why do you have two rooms?"

"I have three, actually."

I lead Charlotte to the door that connects to the adjoining room. After entering *that* one I lock the door behind us, because this is how I live. While I'm nearly positive General Barry's eight-million-dollar job is for real, I can't rule out the possibility he only needed me to kill Chuck, and now that I have, Charlotte could be part of a plot to kill me.

I ask if she has some information for me.

"I do," Charlotte says. "But I'm supposed to make you happy first."

"If you don't mind, I'd like to hear the information first."

She cocks her head. "Business before pleasure? *Really*? How come?"

"Because if there *is* no information, I'll have reason to be concerned. And I'm not a very trusting person to begin with."

Charlotte laughs. "No *kidding* you're not! I've never seen *anyone* with three rooms before! You must be terrified your wife's gonna catch you cheating."

"Tell me the message."

"Okay. The lady who booked me said to give you a message from a man you can trust. She said if I told you that you'd know who the man is." She looks up at me. "Do you?"

I nod.

"His message is you went fishing years ago, just the two of you, and on that day, you caught something other than fish. That's your clue where to find the packet. And when you do, remember the name Sloan."

"Is that the entire message?"

"Yes. Except that the lady wanted me to make it clear you can never call this man, ever again, for any reason."

I make her repeat the message, and she does, with no changes.

Charlotte says, "Can I be honest with you?"

"Please."

"I just want to put it out there that you're the most incredible-looking man I've ever been with."

"Thank you."

"I'm not just saying that. You believe me, don't you?"

"No."

She looks surprised. "Why not?"

"Because you haven't been with me yet."

She grins. "Ah! Well, we can overcome that technicality right now, if you'd like!"

"I'd love to! Unfortunately, I'm not sure I'm ready."

"Why not?" she asks, removing her top.

"It may be too soon."

She wriggles out of her pants. "Try not to think about your wife. This is *our* time. You *deserve* it!"

I pause. I wish I could tell Charlotte the truth: that I'm not ready for sex because I was shot in the chest three months ago and am lucky to be alive. But because the general's aide hired her, I expect she'll be debriefed within hours after leaving my room. So, whatever happens tonight, and whatever information Charlotte uncovers about me will be repeated right up the chain of command. She already knows about the three rooms I reserved, and that information will be recorded and parsed. But if she were to see my bandaged chest, or the grimace on my face if we get physical, the general might decide to have me killed after I complete the upcoming task, or worse, he might conclude I'm physically incapable of doing the job in the first place.

On the other hand, it's been months since I've been with a woman, and this one just got completely naked…on all fours…on the bed…and her ass looks tighter than a bull's butt in fly season.

As I sift through my thoughts she lowers her head and shows me the view she said was off the table just minutes ago. Then she flips over, spreads her legs, and graces me with a glittering smile, and…

Honestly, she's drop-dead gorgeous.

Don't get me wrong, Charlotte doesn't have to be a perfect specimen to turn me on, since I can find enough beauty in *any* woman to get hard. It's just that Charlotte ticks every box in my raging caveman brain and reminds me why I love women so much: they're so different. So beautiful. So…*fuckable*! While all humans share the same 20,000 genes of DNA, the gender differences are specifically tied to the sex chromosomes: women have two X's, men have a single X and a male-specific Y, which makes us more closely related to chimpanzees than to women. So again, while *all* women are beautiful, Charlotte's double-X chromosomes are the product of divine intervention.

And I want her so bad I'm leaking.

You probably think the smart move is to thank her for her time and send her home, but you'd be wrong because the general's quite aware of my fondness for high-class hookers, and knows I'm recently divorced. Rejecting Charlotte would be so out of character it would raise more eyebrows than my chest injury. Which is why I step out of my shoes, remove my socks, and tell Charlotte she's too good to pass up. She grins and says, "Fantastic! Come and get it, Cowboy!"

I step out of my pants and underwear and say, "If you don't mind, I'd prefer to do it standing up."

This doesn't seem to bother her in the slightest, she just needs clarification. "You want me up against the wall?"

I nod.

She scrambles to her feet, moves to the nearest wall, and waits for me to join her. We kiss, and she slides down and warms me up with her mouth. As she looks up at me I instantly respect her for not lying to me, because this is the moment most hookers would have remarked how well-endowed I am.

And I'm not.

If I'm any bigger than average, it's not enough to inspire conversation, but most escorts assume men require validation, so they lie. "Oh, you're so *big*!" they gush, as if size makes all the difference.

It doesn't.

As I've said many times, it's not the size of the sword that counts, it's the fury of the attack. Except that tonight there's only so much I can do without hurting myself, so when Charlotte gets to her feet I have her face the wall and do my best to let her know I'm inside her, though it's hardly momentous.

Afterward, she says, "I know why you did that."

"Tell me."

"You love your wife too much to share the intimacy of a bed, or look into my eyes while we did it. You held back."

"I'm sorry I wasn't better."

"No, it was fine, really. I'm saying I understand, Donovan, and I respect your feelings, and...I'd love to see you again and again, if you'd like."

In my experience there are three types of upper-quality hookers. The worst is the bored, eye-rolling, don't-kiss-me, I-can't-wait-till-this-is-over, I'm-doing-you-a-favor type of girl; the best is the young, eager, "girlfriend-experience" type who kisses you on the mouth, does pretty much whatever your girlfriend would, and works hard to earn her money. The third is the slightly older, more-professional type that holds you close, kisses your cheek, murmurs in your ear, gets you off expertly, and lingers afterward in case you want some conversation, empathy, or just a friendly, non-judgmental ear.

Charlotte's the third type, which is exactly what I'd expect, since General Barry would never trust the bored hooker, or the young hooker, to deliver such an important message. Now, getting dressed, she says, "Honestly, Donovan, I've never met anyone this good-looking before. When I first saw you, I thought you were that famous movie star."

"Which one?"

"I can't remember his name. But your wife must be so proud to be on your arm."

When I fail to respond she says, "Is she incredibly gorgeous?"

"She is. But we're divorced."

"You don't have to say that if it's not true."

"It's true. The divorce was finalized two months ago."

"Wow," she says, as if this information explains a lot.

I cock my head.

She says, "I guess it's true what they say: no matter how gorgeous a guy's wife is, he'll eventually get tired of fucking her."

"Actually, it's just the opposite."

"What do you mean?"

"Guys never get tired of fucking their gorgeous wives. They get tired of *not* fucking them."

I hand Charlotte a five-hundred-dollar tip and when she leaves I stand in the hallway and watch her perfect ass sway gently from side to side all the way to the elevator, while wishing I hadn't been shot.

Chapter 5

ALTHOUGH I CHARGED the hotel rooms to my credit card, Charlotte's tip reduces my cash position to four grand, give or take, which makes this the perfect time to collect the 75k Sal Bonadello owes me for the Rocco hit. But when I get him on the phone he says, "I already paid you."

"What do you mean?"

"I wired the money to your numbered account, same as always."

"Fuck!"

He pauses. "What's wrong?"

"That account's been hacked."

"You should have said something."

He's right. I should have. I'm completely off my game. "Any chance you can cancel the wire?"

"Not really. I sent it before you did the job."

"Fuck! I needed that cash!"

"Geez, that's tough," he says, with a voice entirely unencumbered by empathy. "But if you're really strapped I got a small, but—whatchacall—fortuitous, opportunity if you're in town."

"Which is what, exactly?"

"Rocco's wife, Jessica."

"What about her?"

"I need someone to kill her dog."

"Why?"

"The bastard bit me when I went to pay my condolences."

"How much?"

"Twenty stitches."

"I meant, how much to kill the dog?"

"Fifteen hundred."

"You should have killed it yourself."

"I would, but there's—whatchacall—extenuatin' circumstances."

"I'll do it for ten grand."

"It's a fuckin' *dog*, Creed. I can get one a' my guys to do it for free."

"Fifteen hundred you say?"

"Yeah. And only because the cops are investigatin' Rocco's death. You in town?"

"No, but I can be there by ten tomorrow morning."

"Good. Come to my office," he says, and hangs up.

This is nuts. Can I really have fallen so far that I've agreed to murder a dog for fifteen hundred bucks?

The short answer's yes. And it's even worse than it sounds, because I'm in D.C., Sal's in Cincinnati, and the dog's in Dayton, which means I'll be lucky to break even after paying for my flight and rental car.

So why do it?

Because Rocco was Sal's underboss for many years, which means he had to be a top earner. Since he was talking to the Feds about witness relocation, I'm sure he had a substantial amount of cash saved up for his new life. If so, it's hidden in his house...and Jessica knows where it is.

Chapter 6

"WHAT'S THE DOG'S name?" I ask, as Sal counts out the cash.

"Spirit Walker," he says.

"I should kill Jessica for naming it that."

He laughs. "You should hear her calling the fucker: 'Here, Spirit Walker! Sit, Spirit Walker! Don't bite, Spirit Walker.' But he bites like a motherfucker. Check this out."

He shows me his leg.

I do a double-take. "How big *is* that dog?"

"Huge. He's a—whatchacall—freak a' nature. First time I saw him, I thought he lost his saddle."

"You need to have someone look at that wound."

"I already did. You should a' seen it before."

Out of respect, I wait several seconds before changing the subject. Then say, "You might be missing an opportunity."

"What do you mean?"

"Since I'm already going to Jessica's house for the dog, why not make it a double? I'll give you a discount."

"Why the fuck would I want *Jessica* dead?"

"Are you kidding? She and Rocco were married for twenty years. She's bound to know plenty about his business, including numbers, names and faces. And the Feds already talked to Rocco, so you know they'll be talking to her this week."

He gives me a look. "Jessie's off limits."

"Why?"

"I've been fucking her."

I stare into his eyes a long time before returning his cash.

"What's wrong?"

"I changed my mind."

He studies my face. "Why?"

"I only said yes to the dog because I figured you'd pay me to kill Jessica."

"You sure?"

"Why else would I come all this way for fifteen hundred bucks?"

"That's what I was wonderin'. Maybe you were plannin' to rob her."

I frown. "What sort of man would rob a widow and her kids?"

"The same type who'd kill her for a discount."

"I'd do it to protect you. And whether you're fucking her or not, she's a risk."

"That's my worry, not yours. And anyway, Jessica's—whatcha call—on board."

"Glad to hear it."

"What's goin' on with you? I never seen you hustlin' for money. You in a bind?"

"It's temporary."

"I'm here for you. You know that, right?"

I laugh. "Yeah. But no thanks."

"How come?"

"Your loans don't come with strings attached. They come with ropes."

He grins. "Ropes! I like that!"

"Call me if something comes up."

"Don't I always?"

As I walk away he hollers, "Long as you're here, you should kill the dog!"

I lift my hand and wave without turning around. No way I'm going to kill a dog for fifteen hundred bucks. I genuinely like dogs. To me, they're like kids. And like kids, I go out of my way to avoid killing them.

So...more bad news. Sal's fucking Jessica, so I can't steal her dead husband's stash. And if I kill her and steal it Sal will know it was me. I take a moment to wonder if Sal already took her cash, then decide he hasn't. In fact, he probably let her keep the cash and is paying her to fuck him. Sal says there's nothing to worry about with Jessica, which tells me she's been fucking him for a while.

I think about that for a few minutes and come to the conclusion Jessica's the one who told Sal that Rocco was talking to the Feds. Any bets on whether she increased Rocco's life insurance after she started dating Sal?

Just sayin'...

Chapter 7

IN THE OLD days (last year) I could make a call in any major city and an agency car would show up within minutes. I'd be greeted by a professional, highly-skilled driver who'd know his or her personal life had just been put on hold. They'd be on the clock every moment I needed them, and could have no contact with friends or relatives until I released them. They knew never to speak of anything that transpired during our time together. If they divulged who I was, what I did, where they took me, or what they heard me say, they were putting their lives in jeopardy. Every encounter was treated as a national security event. This, because I'm the head of Sensory Resources, a secret division of Homeland Security that assassinates suspected terrorists before they can attack U.S. targets.

Mostly, I used the cars to take me to the nearest Sensory jet. While it's true I took advantage of the jet privilege and used the fleet for my personal entertainment on numerous occasions, it's also true I helped save more than 100,000 American lives and billions of dollars in property damage over the course of my service, even though I was never paid a dime for it. And since terrorism never sleeps, wherever I went on personal business often put me closer to suspected terrorist activity anyway.

While Sensory Resources never received direct government funding, my boss, Darwin—and later General Barry—always managed to siphon about a billion dollars a year from slush funds and wasteful, unproductive government programs. It wasn't legal, but neither is terrorism, and the results more than justified the theft.

Although I never received direct payment for my service, my bosses allowed me to keep whatever assets I uncovered, which is how I amassed a billion-dollar fortune. It's also the reason why, when you turn on the news and see that a terrorist ring has been destroyed, they never mention the government recovering any cash or bearer bonds.

But those days are over. I'm still the head of Sensory Resources, but the fleets of cars and drivers are gone, and all but three of the jets have been sold, and access to them requires full disclosure and hours of pre-planning. For this reason, I now have to arrange and pay for my transportation in real time, same as you. I'm not complaining, but how would your family feel if the building you're working in gets blown off the map because I couldn't catch a fucking ride to your city in time to stop a terrorist act?

That said, I do have my own personal fleet of private aircraft. *Fleet* might be an exaggeration, since, like Sensory Resources, I only have three: two jets and a helicopter. It's just that I can't afford to fuel them at the moment, which is why I'm sitting in a mid-sized rental car, motoring to Virginia, making calls along the way.

My first call was to Anson, my majordomo, who updated me on the number of workers who are on standby, hoping to get their jobs back. I told him to hire the twelve we need the most for security, and to tell the others I'm hoping to restore their jobs, plus back pay, within 30 to 60 days. Anson was thrilled to hear it and asked if there was anything he could do to help me. I told him to meet me in Moneta and bring two drones, two sets of waders, fishing gear, and enough food and water to last us three days.

"We're going fishing?"

"In a manner of speaking."

"You want waders at Smith Mountain Lake? That's bass fishing."

"Quite right."

He pauses. "Shall I bring backup, Sir?"

"I think we can handle it."

"The two of us?"

"Yes."

"May I assume we'll need firepower?"

"We might."

"What should I bring?"

"Surprise me."

I tell him when and where to meet and he asks no further questions. As I steer my rental car toward Bedford County, Virginia, I get a call from my daughter's legal guardian, Rose Stout.

"How's Hawley?" I say.

"Making progress."

"In what way?"

"Controlling her temper."

This is good news, since it's the primary reason I sent Hawley to live with Rose. The other was my desire for her to have the safest, most normal life possible. To protect her from my enemies, I hired an independent hacker, a kid named Dillon, to manipulate her birth records to reflect that Rose and a dead guy are her birth parents.

Why did I choose Rose?

I trust her. But more importantly, she—like Hawley—is a witch. Not a witch in the sense that they're ugly and wear black clothes and pointy hats and shoes, or chant incantations or spells, or cook with caldrons and fly around on broomsticks. I call them witches because they possess unexplainable super powers.

I'm not talking about the kind of superhuman powers you've read about like the man who can hold his breath underwater for 22 minutes, or the guys who are impervious to pain, or freezing temperatures, or the one who can run 80 hours nonstop on a treadmill without getting tired. Compared to Rose and Hawley, those are parlor tricks. But that doesn't mean they can turn people into newts, or shape-shift, or read people's thoughts, or assume their identities.

But the things they *can* do are much more impressive.

And sometimes terrifying.

For example, as a very young child, Hawley once summoned a quarter-million snakes to our Virginia estate. Before you start doubting, keep in mind, this event was fully documented by local, state, and even national news agencies at the time. No, they didn't attribute the snakes to Hawley, thank goodness. Scientists called it "an extremely rare natural occurrence," and noted that even though they couldn't explain it, similar things have happened before, like on January 15, 1877, when hundreds of people in Memphis, Tennessee, reportedly saw thousands of snakes falling from the sky.

Rose did that. Except she says the snakes were never airborne. "That would be terribly cruel," she said. Apparently, the rain was relentless that day, and the citizens of Memphis couldn't see more than a few feet in front of them. But they *could* see the snakes covering every square inch of a four-block area, so they assumed it was raining snakes.

If you're doing the math from 1877 to the present, you'll find it impossible to believe that Rose could summon snakes that year and is still among us. But what you need to know about Rose is, by the age of ten, she began aging at a much slower rate than the rest of us. Which is why she's more than 300 years old and appears to be 30.

We don't know if Hawley will age the same way. In Rose's considerable lifetime she claims to have met several witches, but none had the innate power to slow their aging. Then again, witches, like magicians, have their own specialties. As clever as Rose is, there are things Hawley can do that Rose can't. For example, Rose can't stare at your face and make your head explode. But Hawley can, as could her great-great-great-grandmother, Scarlett Rose Love-Rennick, who grew up in Dodge City, Kansas, the daughter of a local sheriff named Emmett Love.

My great-great-grandfather.

But that's a whole other story. I'd tell it, but Rose just told me something I can't comprehend. I ask her to repeat it. She says, "Hawley wants to appear on *America Loves Talent*."

"What's that?"

"A TV talent show."

"What talent does she want to do?"

"Magic."

"Fuck."

"Exactly."

Chapter 8

IF I CAN give you a hundred reasons why Hawley shouldn't do "magic" in public, Rose can give you a thousand. And yet she seems open to the idea. When I ask why, she says, "Hawley's not spoiled, but she's willful."

"What does that mean?"

"You don't know?"

"I know what it means when describing a *normal* kid, but—"

"Right. Well, let's just say if she's dead set on doing this, there's not much we can do about it."

"*You* can't stop her?"

"I can try. But I also want to keep my head on my shoulders."

As I drive, I try to imagine it. "What's the worst that could happen?"

"Are you being serious?"

"Yeah."

"If the audience doesn't like her," Rose says, matter-of-factly, "she might kill them."

"I thought you said she was making progress with her temper."

"She is. But she's also a child, on stage in front of thousands of people. She could experience a flood of different emotions. What if her performance goes badly?"

"That's not likely, is it?"

"Who knows? If she happens to get embarrassed and the audience laughs at her she might lash out at them."

"I admit Hawley's a handful, but people love her."

"They do. Generally."

"Then why would anyone laugh at her performance?"

"I doubt they would. They're far more likely to be terrified, depending on what she does to them. Also, one of the judges can be a bit saucy."

"What does *that* mean?"

"It means he can be an asshole."

"To a little *kid*?"

"Yup."

"That'd be a mistake."

"I agree."

I sigh. "Keep trying to talk her out of it, okay?"

"I'll do my best."

"Thanks. Where is she now?"

"On the roof."

"Can I talk to her?"

"She's in a mood. Maybe next time."

"Hi Papa."

"Hawley?"

"I'm on the roof."

Rose says, "How are you on this call?"

"I just am. Did you tell Papa I'm going to be on television?"

"I told him you *want* to, not that you're *going* to."

"Well, I am. It'll be fun."

"Hawley?" I say. "You know I love being your dad, right?"

"I know you *sometimes* do."

"Always."

"Not when you're with Trudy."

"Well, Trudy's gone."

"I know."

"She left months ago. And no one knows where she is."

"*I* do."

I pause. "What do you mean?"

"I know where she is. Want me to say?"

"No. But my point is, you shouldn't call me Papa any more. It's not safe."

"You're afraid of the bad people?"

"No. But I'm afraid they might hurt you."

"How can they hurt *me*?"

Rose says, "They can *burn* you."

Hawley says, "Papa? You got shot. Why didn't you tell me?"

"It was just a scratch."

"Does *this* hurt?"

"*Shit! Jesus Christ!* What the–"

"I just gave you a poke."

"Your poke made me double up in pain."

"It's not just a scratch, Papa."

"No."

"You should always tell me when you get hurt."

"Why?"

"I can make you better."

"How?"

"I'll send healing thoughts every day."

"Thank you. But Hawley?"

"Yes, Papa?"

"Don't ever poke me like that, ever again."

She giggles. "Ready for a healing thought?"

"Sure."

Something...happens. I'm not sure what, or how, but I remember when she was an infant, people used to show up by the hundreds, wherever she was. If she was in a building they'd stand outside like statues until she left. They didn't know who she was, or what was causing them to feel progressively better. They just knew something was drawing them to that particular location. But whatever Hawley did to me just now improved my wound by at least fifty percent. I put the phone down, lift my shirt, remove the tape, and check myself in the closest mirror.

The difference is amazing! Three more days of this and I'll be good as new. I get back on the phone and say, "Hawley, that was truly wonderful. Are you really going to send me a healing thought every day?"

"Yes, Papa. Every night before I go to bed."

"Bless your heart. But as your dad, can I tell you something? It's probably too dangerous for you to be on TV."

"Too bad," she says, "'cause my mind's made up. I'm going."

Like Rose said, she's willful.

Chapter 9

YOU MAY KNOW Smith Mountain Lake: thirty-eight miles from Roanoke, surrounded by mountains, it was featured in the 1991 comedy *What About Bob*, starring Bill Murray and Richard Dreyfuss. The movie misidentified it as Lake Winnipesaukee, an actual lake in New Hampshire, where author John Locke attended summer camp as a boy, 1.35 million years ago.

If I were an author this would be a perfect place to pad my word count with descriptive elements of Smith Mountain's flora and fauna (short version: there are lots of both). I'd make you suffer through thousands of words about how photogenic the lake is in the various seasons (it's a lake, okay? It's pretty all year round). I'd tell you it's only 40 miles long but boasts more than 500 miles of shoreline, including dozens of secluded coves you should hear about. But since I'm not an author, and merely a killer-for-hire, I'll just say there are only two coves that matter: the one where the local librarian lost her virginity at the age of thirty-two (Barber Cove) and the one where, years ago, General Barry hired me to kill his son-in-law.

The librarian, whose name escapes me, was blonde, with unremarkable tits and a fearsome overbite. Or maybe that was

General Barry's son-in-law. It's hard to remember, as I was killing and fucking at such a furious clip in those days. But I do remember that the general and I attempted to fish that day, and the water was selfish, yielding two undersized bluegills and a waterproof boot.

The same boot Anson and I have been seeking for hours.

Earlier today, he and I launched the drones to surveil the area for snipers. Finding none, I canvassed the shoreline for a half hour while Anson stood guard. Not that I expected to find the boot on dry land, but how stupid would I have felt had we spent hours in the water only to find it later, under a bush? Having confirmed my original assumption, we climbed into our waders and began the painstaking process of baby-stepping our way back and forth through the water, stopping constantly to retrieve rocks, cans, sticks, and the occasional bottle, all of which we threw onto the shore. Two minutes ago, after hours of searching, Anson finally held up an object and said, "Is this it?"

It was, and that brings us to present time.

As Anson stands guard, I remove the plastic-wrapped contents and find four keys and a cell phone. Thinking the cell phone could be a bomb, I carefully dismantle it, then reassemble it and check the contact list. Among the three dozen generic ladies' names and numbers, I notice a Sloane. I dial the number, and a woman answers, saying, "Please don't identify yourself. While I have every reason to believe this line is secure, we should never assume it. Please feel free to speak or ask questions, but if you do, disguise your voice. How many keys did you find? Please press the corresponding number on your phone."

I press the number four.

"Excellent," she says. "Each key opens a locker in a different city. In each locker you'll find a bag containing a phone and two million dollars in cash. When you use the phone to verify your identity, we'll tell you where to find the next locker."

Disguising my voice, I say, "Should I call you Sloane?"

"You may call me any name that suits you."

"Thanks. So, Sloane, here's the thing: I'll require full payment in advance."

She laughs. "You sound like that cartoon character," she says. "SpongeBob."

"I was going for Robert DeNiro."

"In that case, don't give up your day job at the Krusty Krab. As for the money, we'll pay one-fourth up front, the balance afterward."

"That's unacceptable."

"Then don't take the job."

"No problem. Enjoy your day." I click the phone off and wait. A moment later, it rings. When I answer she says, "No one pays 100% up front. What if you fail?"

"That won't happen, and your people know it. It's the reason they chose me for the job."

She pauses. "I can maybe get you half up front."

I take a deep breath. "You know what the most dangerous part of my profession is?"

"Sleeping at night?"

"Guess again."

"Living with yourself?"

"The hardest part's collecting the balance of my fee after the job's done."

"I find that hard to believe."

"Think about it this way: when people give me a $4 million deposit it means three things: they have a major problem, they're desperate for a solution, and they've run out of options. After I solve their problem they wonder if it's easier to kill me than pay the balance."

"Who's going to kill *you*?"

"No one, so far. But back in the days when I accepted deposits I ended up having to kill not only the hitmen they sent for me, but my employers, as well."

After a long pause, she says, "Very well. I'll give you all the locker locations and codes, but make no mistake, you'll be on your own. If you get caught, you're screwed. Understood?"

"Of course. Same dance, new partner. What's the job?"

"You're going to kidnap the president's daughter."

"No problem. Which one?"

She laughs. "Well said, Sir." She laughs some more. Then says, "He's only got one child: Analise."

"Only one that we *know* about. How do you want it done?"

"What do you mean?"

"I assume you have a plan."

"You assumed wrong. But we *do* have her itinerary."

"That'll work."

Chapter 10

WHEN SLOANE TELLS me the president's daughter has planned a week-long Thanksgiving ski vacation in Deer Valley with her immediate family, I can't help but smile: billionaire skiing requires tons of clothes and gear, which means they'll be packing trunks, not suitcases.

"How many Secret Service agents?" I ask.

"No way to know. But if you're aware of the staffing issues, you know they're in crisis."

Sloane's referring to the constant vacations, golf outings, promotional tours, and general globetrotting the president and his family have enjoyed since the election. As a result, they exhausted the Secret Service's annual budget for protection more than three months ago. By July, more than eleven hundred agents had already hit the federally mandated caps for salary and overtime. Unable to secure additional funding through congressional intervention, the agents were given the choice of either quitting or working a crushing schedule without pay for the remainder of the year. Not surprisingly, most of them quit, leaving the Agency severely short-handed. I expect in January, armed with a bigger budget, they'll get the Agency back to full capacity. But until then...the president's family is extremely vulnerable.

Not that the agents were kicking ass at full capacity. Remember the allegations of sexual misconduct? The White House security breaches? If a disabled pedestrian can jump the White House fence on the North Grounds and make his way to the front door of the White House, gain access and overpower the guard in the East Room, imagine what Callie Carpenter and I can do at a ski resort in Deer Valley, Utah!

Sloane says, "Any questions?"

"Just to be clear: you want the daughter kidnapped, not killed."

"That's correct."

"Can I kill the husband and kids?"

"Do you *want* to?"

"I might *have* to."

"We'd prefer you didn't."

I pause. "What's the end game?"

"What do you mean?"

"You obviously don't want Analise dead, or you'd let me kill her at the airport, when she departs her jet and walks across the tarmac. Instead, you want her kidnapped, which is a million times more difficult. For that reason, I need to know how long you want me to keep her, and where you want her released."

"Here's the thing: we *do* want you to kill her."

"When?"

"As soon as possible after the kidnapping. But the body can never be found. It's important the world believes she's alive. Understood?"

"You want to control the news cycle."

"Exactly."

"And the narrative."

Instead of responding she says, "Is there anything else you'd like to ask before I give you the locker information?"

"Yes. I'd like a list of all the agents who'll be making the trip. I'll need their personal records, including photos and detailed physical descriptions, right down to their visible tattoos."

"I'm sorry, but that's not going to happen."

"Don't tell me you can't obtain that information. I know better. The previous administration paid me a fortune to create monthly scenarios about how terrorists could successfully kill the president."

"Then you probably already have the dossiers you need."

"I don't, actually."

I'm being honest here. Quick history: up until 2003 the Secret Service was a division of the Treasury Department. In those days, they were top notch. Quite possibly the finest protection force in the world. Now they're under Homeland Security, which makes them a small fish in a big pond. The heads of Homeland Security know me. I kill suspected terrorists for them. Of course they refused to give me dossiers on their agents! They have almost zero control over my actions, and are well aware I could use that data to manipulate or compromise the agents who protect our country's heads of state. But even if I did have their dossiers from last year, half those agents are gone, and the data for the rest of them would be outdated. Not that it matters to Sloane, who says: "In any event, it's your problem, not ours, so you'll have to find a way around it. Surely you understand why we can't pull classified documents weeks before an event of this magnitude: whether you're successful or not, this is the president's *daughter*! Even a *failed* kidnapping attempt will result in a massive, thorough investigation."

I tell her I understand, and she tells me where to find the money lockers. Just as I'm about to hang up I decide to ask one last question: "Does the president know about the kidnapping?"

Chapter 11

"DID YOU SERIOUSLY just ask me that?" Sloane says.

"Yes. I mean, I'm sure the president doesn't know you want her dead, but I can see why he might have orchestrated a fake kidnapping."

"If you know anything about this President, you'll know he loves his daughter more than anyone or anything in the world. She's his only child. He would *never* put her in danger."

"And that's what you're counting on."

"One last thing," she says. "You'll need to shoot at least one of the guards using the weapon you'll find in the first locker."

"What is it?"

"Hang on a sec." I hear her moving some papers around. Then she says, "All I've got is Type 58. Does that mean anything to you?"

It does, but I'm too busy thinking of the implications to answer her. She ends the call saying, "We're done here. Please destroy this phone immediately and remain professional at all times."

I stare at the phone, slack-jawed, then locate a large rock I can use to smash it. But the more I think about it, the less interest I have in destroying it. After another moment of indecision, I place it in my pocket. Anson approaches and asks, "Everything okay?"

"Everything's fine. We're getting paid."

His face brightens. "May I ask how much?"

"Six million, after expenses."

"Wonderful!" After a moment of silence, he says, "You seem to be deep in thought. Are you sure everything's okay?"

"Yes. I just need some time to think."

"Will you be coming home?"

I nod. "I'll follow you there."

"Excellent."

Of course, everything's *not* okay. The Type 58 weapon Sloane referenced is an assault rifle, a derivative of the Soviet AK-47. At 890 mm it's the longest version of the rifle, twenty millimeters longer than the AK-47. But what really matters is the Type 58 rifle has been manufactured since 1958.

In North Korea.

It's the North Korean Army's weapon of choice.

The general and his cohorts want me to kidnap Analise Compton, the president's daughter, and blame it on the North Koreans. Could they be trying to provoke a war?

PART 2

Punch & Judy

Chapter 1

AS DIRECTED, AMANDA Lockmere parks in the hotel garage, exits her car, and climbs into the back seat of the slate-gray Cadillac Escalade. Opposite her is an older man so handsome he could be a leading actor. She sits and extends her hand.

"Hi, I'm Amanda."

"I'm Punch." He laughs at her expression. "Actually, I'm Paul. But–"

"Everyone calls you Punch," she says.

"Exactly."

To the driver she says, "Hi Robert."

"Hello, Miss Amanda. I'll need to check your handbag."

"Seriously?"

"I'm afraid so." He pulls into a vacant parking space. "Please pass it forward."

She does, and as he inspects the items, one by one, Amanda, embarrassed, says, "Is this really necessary? I have some personal items in there."

"No need to apologize, Miss. I've seen Tampons and panty shields before."

"I'm not apologizing. I'm explaining you're invading my privacy, and I'd like you to stop."

Robert turns to face her. "We've paid each of you $10,000 a month, plus benefits, for years, on the *chance* we might need you to actually do some work one day. Well, today's the day."

"What do you mean?"

"You'll be briefed as we ride."

He continues inspecting the contents and zippered pockets of her handbag until he's satisfied there's nothing to worry about. Then he says, "I'll need your phone, please."

Amanda looks at Punch. "Did you give him yours?"

He nods.

She sighs, hands it over. Robert makes sure it's turned off, then places it carefully in the console. He backs out of the parking space, exits the garage, and works his way to the Interstate before saying, "The job we have for you involves little or no danger. But it must be done precisely as we ask, or there could be repercussions."

"Like what?" Punch says.

"People could die."

Amanda laughs. "That sounds hyperbolic."

Robert says, "I can assure you, this is quite serious."

Amanda's grin disappears. "I won't do anything illegal. I made that crystal clear in the initial interview nearly three years ago."

"You did. And that's not a problem, because we're not *asking* you to do anything illegal." He pauses. "Nevertheless, you may be surrounded by illegal activity, which means if you go off script, people could die."

"Which people?"

"The people who keep our country safe from terrorists."

She pauses. "This sounds bigger than what I signed up for."

"Did I mention the bonus? A thousand dollars a day for each day you're on the job. In addition to your base salary."

Amanda thinks about it. "What would I have to do?"

"Fake a relationship."

She frowns. "What's that supposed to mean?"

"It means later today you and Punch are going to pretend to meet online. Over the next two weeks I'll call both of you daily and dictate carefully-worded messages you'll send to each other. You'll send the exact messages I dictate, with no ad-libbing."

"What type of messages?"

"Flirty. As I said, you're going to fake a relationship. The messages will be designed to establish you as a couple in the fastest-possible manner. After a few days, you'll meet, start dating, and post photos on your social media accounts. After two weeks you'll do a weekend vacation together. You'll introduce each other to your parents and friends, and take photos and post them. You'll tell your friends and family you're crazy about Punch, and he'll tell his friends and family the same about you. You'll go on one or two trips together, having fun, posting pictures, all at our expense. It's basically a dream job."

"Are you saying I have to sleep with this guy? No offense, Paul, but I'm twenty-six. And you must be what, forty-five?"

"Close. I'm forty-four."

"You could be my father."

"You think?"

"You're eighteen years older than me. Do the math."

"If you really think it's a possibility, I suppose we can ask your mom."

"No need to be sarcastic. My point is I'm not having sex with a total stranger, especially one who's nearly twice my age."

"What happens in your hotel room is up to you," Robert says. "But in public, at all times, you're going to interact as if you're very much in the budding stages of love. That means hugging, kissing, and lots of smiles. Are you up for it?"

"No."

"Punch?"

"Sir?"

"How about you?"

"Absolutely."

"Excellent."

Robert turns off the Interstate at the next exit and drives until they get to a boarded-up gas station. He pulls into the vacant lot and parks.

"What now?" Amanda says.

"Your ride's here."

She looks out the window and sees an identical Escalade parked beside them. When the back-seat door opens, a lady climbs out. Amanda's eyes go wide. Punch says, "She looks like your twin sister!"

"She does indeed," Robert says. "Only prettier."

The blonde opens Amanda's door and says, "Don't worry, Amanda. You don't have to do anything that makes you uncomfortable."

"Who are you?"

"I'm the one."

Chapter 2

"WHAT DO YOU mean?" Amanda asks.

The blonde says, "You were hired years ago because you resembled me. But we have others, so you needn't worry. I'll give you a ride back to your car."

"How did...I mean, have you been listening to our conversation this whole time?"

"We have. And we agree this is more than you bargained for."

"Does this mean I'm fired?"

"Sadly, yes."

"But I really need the money! Is there anything else I can do? I'm only declining sharing a hotel room with a man and faking a public romance."

"Can I ask why that's so difficult for you?"

Amanda smiles. "I'm recently engaged."

The blonde looks at Robert, then back at Amanda. "That was specifically prohibited."

"*Why*? I mean, for two years people with the company called me at least once a week, and I always abided by the rules. Then the calls stopped, and I haven't heard from anyone since December. I assumed the rules had changed."

"And yet you continued cashing the paychecks."

"Yes, but–"

"It's okay, we don't expect a refund. But you'll need to come with us."

Amanda looks at Robert for support. Getting none, she asks, "Why?"

"You've put us behind schedule, and now Robert and Punch have to drive all the way to Indianapolis to meet with your replacement."

"You found someone else who looks like you and me?"

"Several."

"And you've been paying *them* all this time, *too*?"

"Longer, actually."

"If you have all those others, why did you choose *me*?"

"We chose Punch because we trust him to do everything we ask, and we chose you because you're local. It's just logical your relationship with Punch would build faster if you're both local. But it's okay. We'll work it out. Let's go."

Amanda bites her lip. "I'm not leaving this car."

For Punch, it makes no sense. One second he's watching two gorgeous twins having a discussion, and the next, he's retching uncontrollably, sitting in his own shit. This, because without changing her facial expression, the evil twin just snapped Amanda's neck and dragged her out of the car.

It was crazy. And sickening, the sound her neck made, and the way her feet twitched afterward.

Now, as Robert puts the SUV in drive and casually exits the vacant lot, he says, "It appears you'll need a change of clothes." Stopping at the first gas station they come to, he says, "I'm sorry you had to see that just now. But like I told Amanda earlier, we take our work very seriously." He turns around in his seat to look at Punch. "I know you're upset, concerned about your safety, but please believe me: other than asking you to tell the occasional lie, we'll never ask you to break any laws. If you always do whatever we ask, I'll *personally* guarantee your safety. You have my word. Okay?"

Punch nods.

"Excellent. Now go in the bathroom and get yourself as clean as you can. While you're doing that, I'll clean the vehicle and swing by Wal-Mart to get you some clean clothes. Stay in the bathroom till I get back. Any questions?"

"Um…about Amanda. I mean, is…is she–"

"Is she dead? I certainly hope so, for *her* sake. Anything else?"

"N-No, Sir."

Two hours later Robert and Punch pull into a hotel parking garage in downtown Indianapolis. When the door opens, it's like déjà vu, except that the identical young lady extending her hand says, "Hi. I'm Judy."

Punch looks at Robert.

Robert nods.

Punch takes her hand, smiles as warmly as his fear permits, and says, "Hi, Judy, I'm Punch."

As she enters the SUV, Punch finds himself hoping Judy's going to be up for whatever.

Chapter 3

TO JUDY, THE job sounds simple enough. All she and Punch have to do is pretend to meet in a chatroom, type out the emails they're given each day on the burner phones Robert provides, and pretend to develop a romance. In a week they'll meet for a dinner date, post photos on their social media accounts, and step up the chats. Make phone calls. Have more pretend dates. Then a weekend together, at a resort.

First issue: introducing Punch to her parents.

Judy says, "I'm not sure my parents will approve of the age difference."

"Paul's a classy guy," Robert says. "You might be surprised. But you need to try, since a photo with the parents will help sell the romance." He continues outlining the process: more photos, more social media interaction. Possibly another weekend getaway. And then...

A week-long Thanksgiving ski trip, in Deer Valley, Utah.

Second issue: the date. Judy's never missed Thanksgiving Dinner with her parents.

"Find a way," Robert says.

Third issue: the event.

"The Deer Valley trip is the real thing," Robert says. "This is where the event will take place."

"Which event?" Judy asks.

"You don't want to know."

"Why not?"

"Because the only way you can be truly innocent is if you don't know anything. As for the rules, you'll both be required to wear specific clothes each day. You won't be allowed to leave your room, or order room service, without permission. Your job is to be seen, but not to engage with people unless we ask you to. Can you both ski?"

"I'm pretty good," Punch says.

"I can do Intermediate slopes," Judy says.

"Good. Some days you might ski, some days we might have you stay in the room. We might have you watch certain people and report on their activities. Other than that, you'll act as if you're two lovebirds, having a fun vacation."

"What if people ask questions?"

"You can tell the truth about everything except us."

"What if they ask about our jobs?"

"You both work for actual corporations, where you're listed as outside consultants. If anyone contacts the companies for verification, they'll get it."

"How's that possible?" Judy asks.

"Our team of consultants have been doing your work off-site for years." He smiles. "You do excellent work, by the way."

Judy looks at Punch. "Why are you so quiet?"

"What do you mean?"

"Don't you have any questions?"

"No. I'm just grateful to get paid a fortune for looking like someone else."

"Doesn't it bother you that the people we look like might be committing serious crimes?"

Punch looks at Robert. Then says, "No. Because they work for Homeland Security, and whatever they're doing is keeping the country safe."

Judy frowns. "But how do we *know* that?"

Punch says, "Because I met the one that looks like you. And I trust her."

"Are you sure?"

"Totally."

Robert smiles. "What do you say, Judy? Are you in?"

She looks at Punch. He nods encouragingly.

"Let's do it," he says. "It'll be fun. Not only that, but we're helping our country."

"Assuming they're not killing people and setting us up to take the blame."

"That's not going to happen," Robert says.

"Convince me."

"It's simple: like I said, you don't know anything. You also have no Homeland Security background, no knowledge of how to do what's going to happen, and you probably wouldn't even be able to answer a single question anyone might ask about the events that are going to unfold. And your stories will check out: you're normal people leading normal lives who met online and fell in love."

Judy thinks about it a moment, then says, "You said something about a daily bonus, but you didn't quote a figure."

"One thousand a day, plus expenses."

"In *addition* to my salary?"

"That's correct."

She grins. "You should have said that up front. I'm in!"

"Are you certain?"

"Yup. If you're paying me this much money, and I don't have to commit any crimes, you can kill the president, for all I care."

"I hope it goes without saying you can't mention this to anyone. Not even each other."

"Why not each other?" Punch says.

"You can never know who might be listening."

PART 3

Callie & Creed

Chapter 1

LOCATED JUST EAST of Park City, Utah, Deer Valley is consistently rated among the top ski resorts in the world. The topmost run hits an altitude of 9,570 feet, and the longest is a staggering three miles. Features include luxury accommodations, gourmet restaurants, a world-class ski school, and 101 ski runs that are strictly limited to 7,500 skiers per day.

Waiting for the Comptons to descend the upper portion of an expert slope would be the ideal (and most obvious) place to kill the Secret Service agents, disable Randy, drug Analise, pack her in a snowmobile, and rush her off the mountain to a waiting four-wheel-drive vehicle. Here's why:

1. Cell phone reception on the mountains is spotty to non-existent, which means the agents might have trouble calling for backup when the shooting starts.
2. Analise and her husband, Randy, are expert skiers, so they'll ski the most difficult and least crowded slopes, which means I'd have a good chance of securing and settling into a decent shooting location without being detected.

3. Their kids won't be skiing with them on the expert slopes.
4. Only the smallest percentage of Secret Service agents can ski at the Compton's level, so there would probably be only one or two agents accompanying them down the slopes.

But I'm not going to kidnap her at the top of a ski slope. I'm going to do it in the most difficult and least obvious place possible: her hotel room.

Not because I think the general's setting me up to be killed during an attempted kidnapping, but because if I try to whisk Analise off the mountain in broad daylight I'd be easy to track because Deer Valley doesn't allow snowmobiles on their slopes (I'd have the only one), and because the Secret Service, though understaffed, will certainly have helicopter support standing by in case of a security threat or in the event the Comptons or their kids suffer an accident requiring immediate medical treatment. While I like the fact that cell coverage is poor and I'd only have to deal with killing a couple of Secret Service agents, I don't like my chances of getting Analise off the mountain.

There's also the problem of having to shoot one of them with a Type 58 assault rifle. After all, they don't come equipped with silencers. And even if they *did*, this isn't Hollywood. In real life, silencers only reduce the sound of a gunshot by roughly 14% to 19%. In other words, even with silencers, guns are crazy loud.

Especially assault weapons.

With all this in mind, I called my top assassin, Callie Carpenter, and asked her to meet me in Deer Valley.

When she arrives, I describe the job, give her a million dollars, and walk her through my plan. When she fails to comment, I ask what's wrong.

"I'm waiting for the punchline."

"It's not a joke," I say. "That's the plan."

"You need to scrap it."

"You have a better idea?"

"I do. We should target Analise and Randy while they're skiing down an expert ski slope." I wait respectfully while she enumerates all the reasons I've already considered. Then I tell her about the helicopter, and how snowmobiles are prohibited on the mountains, and she laughs and says, "You failed to mention the obvious problem: you don't ski."

"*I* don't, but *you* can, and anyway, I'd be on the snowmobile, remember?"

"Yeah. But good luck trying to walk around in boots on an expert slope. You'll get bogged down before you get ten feet."

"All the more reason to do it right here, in the Presidential Suite."

"Which brings up a good point. How can you be certain they'll stay in this room?"

"It's the *Presidential* Suite. Where *else* would they stay?"

"In a ski-in, ski-out, six-bedroom condo."

"Why?"

"It would allow eight agents to sleep in four of the bedrooms, while eight more secure the perimeter and maintain security."

"They won't have anywhere close to sixteen Secret Service agents on Thanksgiving week."

"How many are you expecting?"

"Six to eight, max."

"That's crazy!"

"Two to accompany Randy and Analise on the slopes, two to keep an eye on the kids at ski school, and two to secure this very room: one outside the door, the other twenty yards away, by the elevator."

"And at night?"

"Two sleeping next door, two in the hall, one in the entertainment area of the suite, and one in the lobby."

"So, we'd have to kill all six, possibly eight, deal with the husband and kids, and get Analise down to the lobby and out the door."

"That's right."

"Like I said, it's crazy."

"What's the craziest part, in your opinion?"

"Shooting one of the guards in the middle of the night. This is the top floor. There are two elevators, both of which have cameras. Why are you smiling?"

"You noticed the cameras."

She frowns. "Why wouldn't I?"

"As far as you knew, you were meeting me for lunch. I never told you where the job would take place."

She shakes her head. "Doesn't take much to impress you. Speaking of which, how's Trudy these days?"

"Still alive, far as I know."

"I can solve that for you, if you like."

"I'm moving on."

"You've already found someone?"

"No. But I'm ready to start looking."

She catches my eyes with her gaze. "Maybe you'll fuck Analise."

I want to tell Callie I'd like that, but she has a jealous streak where I'm concerned. She doesn't want me personally, she just doesn't want *other* women to have me. So, I say, "That's not likely."

Without taking her eyes off mine she says, "But you've *thought* about it."

"Not really."

"You don't find her attractive?"

I shrug. "I admit she's hot. But she's certainly not a goddess."

"So, just to be clear...you're *not* interested in fucking her?"

"Not at all," I say, lying through my teeth.

"Can I?" she says.

"Up to you."

"Then...yes," she says. "I'd like that."

"Why?"

"I'd like to rage-fuck her."

"Why?"

"I hate her father."

"That's sexual assault."

"Not if it's consensual."

"I'm pretty sure she's straight."

"They're all straight till they see the curve of my ass."

I laugh. "How long have you been waiting to use that line?"

"Couple of months."

"Did you practice?"

"Yeah. Just now."

"Well, talk all you want, but here's what I know: you, more than anyone I've ever met, live by a code. There's no circumstance under which you'd sexually assault anyone, for any reason."

"I'd shove a grenade up her father's ass."

"No, you wouldn't. Want to check out the bedroom?"

She arches a brow. "All this talk about Analise getting you hot?"

"Don't be silly. I just want to get your opinion."

"On what?"

"The box spring."

"Donovan, look at me. This is the dumbest plan you've ever had."

"Let's not reject it till we've done our homework."

She rolls her eyes. "Whatever. Can I ask you one quick question before we get started?"

"Of course."

"Did you ever fuck Dani Ripper?"

"*That's* your question?"

"Yes."

"No."

"But you *wanted* to, right?"

I give her a look. "Dani's a friend."

"So?"

"She's in a committed relationship."

"So?"

"Why would I want to jeopardize her happiness?"

"Because she's hotter than nine levels of hell and you're perpetually horny."

"*Perpetually*? That seems harsh."

"Let me put it this way," Callie says. "You'd fuck a rockpile, hoping for a snake."

I frown. "Look who's talking. What about you?"

"What *about* me?"

"Did *you* ever fuck Dani?"

"I'll never tell," she says, laughing. Then points at my crotch and says, "You're picturing it right *now*, aren't you!"

I change the subject. "Let's get started. We still need to meet Crazy Alma, in Park City."

"Does this mean I finally get to meet the Preacher?"

"Probably."

"Oh boy!" Callie says, sarcastically.

Chapter 2

ALMA ISN'T REALLY crazy, I just call her that because of her customers. She inherited a boarding house in Park City that over the years became a magnet for troubled adults who are generally sane, but quirky as shit. It's been two years since my last visit, but it's one I'll never forget. I arrived unannounced, while Alma was at the grocery store. So, I sat quietly at her kitchen table to wait for her return. After a few minutes one of her boarders—an old man with Moses hair and bug eyes the size of ping pong balls—took the chair opposite me and said, "All she had to do was lay there and not die."

When I ignored him, he leaned toward me and challenged me to a staring contest.

I moved my chair back to keep some space between us, and asked, "Who died?"

He said, "The audience lady." As if that explained everything.

After further questioning I learned he was a former faith healer and part-time magician who used to work his magic act into his sermons. One night in a revival tent in Grand Junction, Colorado, he preached about how people had become slaves to the clock. "Never enough time to get things done!" he thundered, reliving the sermon.

"Always got to *be* somewhere, always got to be *doin'* something! We're slaves to the clock!"

He called for volunteers and chose a lady from the audience to come up on stage and climb into a grandfather clock that was supposed to turn into a coffin. And all she had to do was lie there and not die. But she had a heart attack, and so the Preacher lost his reputation and livelihood, and eventually wound up in Crazy Alma's boarding house.

Today, Callie and I are sitting at the same kitchen table, waiting on Alma to finish talking to the two police detectives on the front porch.

"Where's the Preacher?" Callie asks.

"Didn't see him."

"I'm talking to *that* guy," Callie says, pointing behind me. I turn and see a man so slim if he was shorter he could pass for an ass crack.

He glares at her. "Payments are due by the 10th of February. No exceptions."

Callie and I exchange a look. She turns back to him and says, "February 10th. Got it. So, where's the Preacher? I'd like to meet him."

For whatever reason, the thin man's severely agitated. He shouts, "It's *imperative* that your garage be, at a *minimum*, a full two feet behind the façade!"

Callie's had enough. "I'll build my garage wherever the fuck I want," she says.

The man's face freezes with fury. "You'll get yours!" he screams.

"Oh yeah?" Callie says. "What are *you* gonna do about it?"

He shows her a smug smile. "I'm taking this issue straight to committee. Consider yourself screwed."

As he rushes from view, Callie hollers, "I've had better!"

A voice behind us says, "Disregard Jonathan. He's stuck in the past. Used to be president of his neighborhood homeowner's association. Thinks he's still in charge. Takes his duties seriously."

I stand to greet Alma, but hugging her is always awkward, since she's four feet shorter than me. I notice her eyes are red and brimming with tears. Callie introduces herself and asks if the Preacher's still living here.

Alma says, "He went missing a week ago. That's why the detectives were here just now."

"It took them a whole *week* to show up?"

"No." She sighs deeply. "They stopped by to tell me they found his body."

"On a happier note," Callie says, "We've got a job for you."

Chapter 3

THOUGH SHE'S WORKED with us in the past, Alma's expertise falls short of murder. Her specialty is surveillance and infiltration, which is a fancy way of saying we stuff her slender, 32-inch-tall body into small, custom-made enclosures, and monitor her texts.

After hearing my plan, Alma says, "You can't be serious!"

Callie laughs.

"So, let me get this straight," Alma says. "You're going to put me inside Analise Compton's luggage, sneak me into her suite, and I'm supposed to text you everything I see and hear."

"Exactly," I say.

"And what happens when they unpack their luggage and find me in it?"

"I think you misunderstood that part of the plan. You're going into the luggage after it's been unloaded."

"That's crazy."

"All plans sound crazy until they work."

She looks at Callie. "Does this plan *ever* sound sane?"

"Not to me."

Alma says, "She's the president's daughter. She's bound to keep her luggage locked. How will I get in it?"

Alma, clearly distracted by the Preacher's death, obviously lost the thread. So I take a deep breath and repeat the plan from the beginning: "The Compton family is comprised of two adults and three children. They're multi-millionaires, and it's a week-long ski vacation, so they'll have more luggage than they can carry on a private jet. For this reason, they'll pack their bags ahead of time and have them shipped to the hotel before their arrival. The day before the family arrives, their butler will show up with three Secret Service agents. Two will accept the keys to the Presidential Suite, and, with the hotel manager present, they'll check the room from top to bottom. When the manager leaves, they'll sweep the room for surveillance equipment."

"Bugs."

"That's right. And while that's happening, the butler and third Secret Service agent will be with a bellman, in the storage area, sorting the family's luggage into two piles. The bags containing skis and ski boots will be sent to the ski storage room, and the others will be taken by bellmen—under the watchful eye of the butler and Secret Service agent—to the Presidential Suite. Once inside the room, the butler will unpack the bags, iron the clothes, put them in drawers or on hangers. Then he'll order the food and drinks the family will want in the kitchen."

"Why's that important?"

"It's not. I just want you to know what will be happening while you're hiding in the bag in the closet."

"What bag in the closet?"

I look at Callie, who shrugs as if to say, "What do you want from me? It's a stupid plan."

To Alma I say, "Remember the second set of bags? The ones containing their skis and boots? There'll be one or two large trunks with boot bags in them, and five ski bags. When those get to storage they'll be opened, and the equipment will be placed in lockers. Then a bellman will put the empty bags into the trunks and take them to the Presidential Suite. Except that I'm going to intercept him, assume his identity, put you in one of the boot bags, put the bag in the bottom of one of the trunks, and take you and the bags to the Presidential Suite."

"You're going to pose as the bellman?"

"That's right."

"Why can't the hotel store the ski bags in the ski storage room?"

"Normally they would. But the Compton's are coming for Thanksgiving week and the storage room will be overloaded. They won't have the space to accommodate all the guests' baggage."

"So, you're going to put me in a trunk, sneak me inside the Presidential Suite, and put me in a closet."

"A closet, or some other out-of-the-way area, and you'll be our eyes and ears inside the suite."

"And how will that help you?"

"Callie and I will be monitoring your texts. You'll hear what the family's plans are, where they're going, and when. You'll hear exchanges between the family and Secret Service. All this information will let us know Analise's plans before the fact. It'll allow us to remain one step ahead of the agents."

"How will I get out of the bag to use the bathroom?"

"When I zip you into the bag I'll leave a two-inch opening. When everyone's out of the suite, you'll put your finger in the opening, slide the zipper, exit the bag, and climb out of the trunk."

"Tell me again about the box spring."

"The Presidential Suite has three areas: far left is the master bedroom. Center is the common space, consisting of a den and dining room. Far right are the guest bedrooms, where the kids will sleep. I'll try to get you in or near the closet of the center section. But wherever you are, if something unexpected happens and you can't get back to the trunk, you'll need a hiding place. So later today you, me, and Callie will go to the master bedroom of the Presidential Suite and carve a three-foot cubby into the box spring, underneath the mattress." I pause. "Any questions?"

"Just one: you don't look like any kind of bellman I've ever seen. What if the agents make you open *all* the bags? What if they see me?"

"If that happens I'll kill them, and you'll run like hell."

Chapter 4

I AGREE IT sounds like a crazy plan, and that's not even the tough part! Getting Alma to keep us posted on the family's whereabouts is only the first step. Callie and I will still have to separate Analise from her family and the Secret Service agents, and kidnap her, and shoot at least one of the agents with the Type 58 North Korean rifle. So, you can imagine my surprise when, hours after Analise and her family arrived at the ski resort, Callie calls my phone asking, "Where are you right now?"

"With Alma. I just subdued the bellman, and we're heading for the elevator."

"You mean it *worked*? She's in the trunk?"

"Don't be a snot. My plans always work."

"*Always*?"

"Usually."

She says, "Stop walking for a minute."

I do as she says. "What's up?"

Callie sighs. "Look. I know you really want to do this your way, but there are a hundred things that could go wrong."

"What's your point?"

"It's an extremely difficult mission that requires a lot of improvisation."

"That's never stopped us before."

"True, but–"

"Callie?"

"Yeah?"

"Do you trust me?"

"Always."

"I got the Secret Service part right."

"You did."

"And the Presidential Suite."

"True."

"And the butler part, and the luggage part, and the family's outside, ice skating, which means the agents are divided, with only one guarding the door of the suite."

"What are you trying to say?"

"Is my plan working so far?"

"Yes."

"Then let's move forward."

For a second, she's silent. Then she says, "What's that squeaking sound?"

"I'm pushing the luggage cart down the hall."

"What floor are you on?"

"Ground. Heading toward the elevator. But I've gotta say, I'm a bit disappointed by your negative comments."

"Sorry."

"Just out of curiosity, why'd you wait till now to express your doubts? We reviewed the plan twenty times, and it's working. I thought you were on board."

"I was."

"So, what's the problem?"

"I already kidnapped her."

I stop short. "*What?*"

"I kidnapped Analise."

"*When?*"

"Minutes ago. While they were ice skating."

"You took her right off the *ice?*"

"Not exactly."

"Did anyone see you?"

"I hope not."

"Where is she now?"

"In the trunk of Alma's car."

"What about her phone?"

"Disabled."

"Where's the car?"

"In front of the hotel."

"You're behind the wheel?"

"Yes."

"And she's in the trunk?"

"That's correct. If you don't mind, could you grab my bag when you get yours?"

"Yeah, sure."

"What's wrong?"

"Nothing."

She pauses. "You're upset I screwed up your plan."

"Don't be silly. But you have to admit it was a great plan. It would've worked."

"It was an *okay* plan. It *might've* worked."

"Guess we'll never know now."

Callie says, "Shall I let her go so you can try it your way?"

"No. Stay put, Smart Ass. I'll get Alma out of the trunk, clean the room, get our clothes, grab the rifle, and shoot the agent."

"Which agent?"

"At this point, who gives a shit?"

"Don't be that way."

I pause. "Sorry. You're right. I've had a chip on my shoulder about the plan from day one. But the truth is, you did a helluva job. You killed it."

"Thanks, Boss."

"I can't wait to hear how you managed it."

"It wasn't that big a deal."

"Don't be modest. I couldn't have done it. Truly, you're amazing. I'm thoroughly impressed."

"Stop. You're making me blush."

"Still, great job. Okay, so I'll put the rifle in one of the ski bags and shoot one of the agents at the skating rink. Then I'll ditch the rifle and work my way back to the car."

"Sounds good."

"After Alma gets in the car, drive around a bit, then look for me. I should be ready in about eight minutes."

"No problem. But Donovan?"

"Yeah?"

"Your orders were to *shoot* an agent, not *kill* one, correct?"

She's right about that. I tell her so.

"Good. Just one shot, okay? Make it a flesh wound."

"Why?"

"I promised Analise no one would get hurt."

With that, she ends the call, so I slide the trunk off the luggage carrier, open it, and release Alma from the boot bag. "I guess you heard what happened."

"What are you talking about?"

"You didn't hear me on the phone just now?"

Alma shakes her head.

"That can't be true! I was right beside you!"

"Sorry. I didn't hear a thing."

"Shit!"

"What's wrong?"

I stare at her. If she didn't hear *me* talking, she never would have heard the family talking in the Presidential Suite. I say, "Do me a favor, okay? Don't tell Callie!"

Chapter 5

NOW, IN THE car, heading to Park City, I ask Callie if Analise is unconscious. She tells me yes, she gave her a sedative after putting her in the trunk.

Alma says, “I can’t believe we spent all that time and effort for nothing.”

I frown. “What are you talking about?”

“The planning, the scouting, the hours we spent keeping tabs on the butler and Secret Service agents. Not to mention the cubby we made in the box spring.”

“We didn’t waste any time at all,” I say. “The mission was successful. In fact, we accomplished it at least a day sooner than expected.”

“Thanks to Callie.”

Noticing the slight smile playing across Callie’s lips I say, “Callie’s improvisation was part of the plan.”

Alma laughs. “I’m sure.”

“You should be happy you didn’t have to sit in a luggage bag all night.”

"I'm *super* happy about that. And to tell you the truth, I wasn't thrilled about being stuck in the box spring, under the mattress. What if I'd been hiding there and Analise and Randy decided to have sex? Or what if the kids decided to jump up and down on the bed? I could've been crushed."

"As it turns out," I say, "The cubby was worth building."

"Why?"

"If they find it while investigating the kidnapping, it'll confuse the hell out of them."

"Why?"

"It's not long enough for the rifle or big enough to hide a suitcase Analise could fit in."

Alma says, "My biggest concern has always been that the cubby might lead them to my door."

"How's that possible?"

"A lot of people noticed me at the hotel these past two days. Plus, my car was parked in the garage for hours at a time. They probably have security cameras. What if they saw Callie put Analise in my trunk? I can't help but think when they find that cubby in the box spring they'll realize it was designed to hide a little person."

"Don't be silly," Callie says. "There are no cameras in the parking garage. We checked. Not only that, but we lined your trunk with plastic tarps, so even if they suspect you, locate you, and check your trunk, they won't find any DNA evidence. And anyway, how could they *possibly* believe you managed to overpower Analise Compton and physically put her in your trunk?"

"That's a good point."

"Don't forget, we were *also* seen there, and unlike you, we were *staying* there. When the Feds ask for descriptions of the couple that went missing around the same time as Analise, don't you think some will remember the beautiful blonde bombshell that no man or woman can resist?"

"I suppose."

"And who was driving your car?"

"You."

"That's right. So, if anyone *does* happen to identify your car, you can say it was stolen by the gorgeous blonde." Noticing the flashers on the side of the road, Callie asks me if that's Anson.

"It is. Go ahead and cross the bridge, then pull over. He'll come to us."

As Callie slows the car and parks on the shoulder, Alma says, "The problem is, regardless of who was driving my car at the hotel, I'll be driving it home. It'll be in my garage in ten minutes."

"No, it won't," Callie says.

"Why not?"

"You need to be able to prove your car was really stolen. Remember, I was sitting behind the wheel in front of the lobby for more than five minutes. If anyone saw you get in the back seat of your own car, it'll help prove your claim. When you get home, you need to immediately file a police report."

"Why?"

"For your protection. You can give them our descriptions, but not our names. I doubt anyone will contact you, but if they do, you'll be able to honestly say you were kidnapped by a stunning beauty and..." She winks at me and adds: "her elderly gentleman friend."

Alma's not in the mood for playful. "You're stealing my *car*?"

"We are," Callie says.

"I can't walk all the way home from here!"

"Why not? It's three miles, max."

"I'm a little person, and it's forty degrees outside. I'm sorry, but this is unacceptable."

I say, "What if we ask Anson to drive you a little closer?"

"A *lot* closer would be better."

"No problem."

When we exit the car, Callie kills Alma while Anson and I transfer Analise to the trunk of his rental car. Then Anson gives us the tiny weighted vest he created for the occasion. While I put it on Alma, carry her to the bridge, and toss her over the guard rail, Callie takes a minute to go through Analise's handbag, then places it in Anson's trunk. I take that moment to phone Punch. When he answers, I say, "You and Judy need to make yourselves visible." Punch says they're already visible, since all hell broke loose at the hotel a few minutes ago.

"What happened?"

"No one knows, but whatever it is, it's big."

"Where are you now?"

"In the parking lot, across from the hotel entrance."

"Why?"

"That's where they sent everyone. There was a fire alarm."

"What's the Secret Service doing?"

"Running around like the Marx Brothers in *Duck Soup*."

"Then I guess it's time to find out if we can trust you guys."

"We're good to go, Boss."

"Good, because it's crunch time. You'll be questioned by Secret Service and possibly the FBI. Does that frighten you?"

"Not really."

"Good. Any last-minute questions?"

"No sir."

"You know what to do?"

"Stick to the story and add nothing."

"Perfect."

Punch says, "Can I ask what happened?"

"It's better if you hear it from someone else. Is Judy close by?"

"She's right beside me."

"Have you banged her yet?"

"No, Sir."

"Have you tried?"

"Nonstop!"

I laugh. "Put her on the phone."

He does, and I hand her off to Callie, who says, "Remember everything I said about what happened in the bathroom?" Pause. "Good. When the Secret Service interviews you I want you to be spunky. Otherwise you'll come across nervous and uptight. Answer all their questions, but don't elaborate. You saw Analise Compton in the restroom, asked for her autograph, and left. A few minutes later, you circled around, came back to try to talk to her again, but the Secret Service agent intercepted you." This entire conversation is news to me. Callie listens for a minute, then says, "don't be afraid to steer the conversation to your boobs." Judy says something, and Callie laughs. "Nope. I had all thongs." She laughs again, and says, "I'll ask him and get back to you. You're gonna do great. I can't wait to hear all about it!"

When she ends the call I say, "Autograph?"

"Yup. I'll explain later."

"I'll look forward to that. Did I also hear you say that Judy spoke to a Secret Service agent tonight?"

"Yeah. He was guarding Analise. I needed to create a diversion, so I could get her from the bathroom to the car. It worked."

"I thought you got her off the ice at the skating rink."

"The *family* was on the ice."

Anson walks over and says, "I like that couple, Punch and Judy. I hope they miss me, playing the part of Robert. I trust everything went well?"

"So far, so good," I say.

Callie says, "Judy said to tell you hi, and she loved our matching wardrobes. Except for the two pair of granny panties. I told her you gave me all thongs. What's up?"

"I considered them more practical for snow skiing."

"Good point."

He bows slightly, and I tell them it's time to get moving.

As Anson drives away with Analise, Callie and I take Alma's car to the Salt Lake City airport and park it in short-term. Then we book an Uber with a driver named Ted, and have him take us to the address we typed into Callie's burner phone, which happens to be a vacant office building. On the way, Ted asks if we're married. After saying we're not, he tells us all about his kids, and says he hasn't seen or heard from them since his divorce.

"What's your ex's name?" Callie asks.

"Miriam."

"She sounds stuffy," Callie says. "I bet she's got small tits and rich parents."

"Very."

"Very which?" she says. "Stuffy? Small tits? Or rich parents."

He chuckles. "All three."

When we get to our destination, I tell Ted to drive around to the back. When he does, I pull a gun on him and tell him to shut off his device to signify he's no longer on duty.

He says, "Are you gonna jack my car?"

"Yes."

"Please don't."

"Sorry, Ted. It's kind of important."

Ted surprises me by blurting out, "I live with my parents."

"At *your* age?" Callie asks. "That's sad as hell. But why are you telling us that?"

"I was hoping you'd feel sorry for me. It's been a tough year. I lost my wife, my kids, my house, and my job."

"How'd you lose your *job*?" I ask.

"I was working for Miriam's father."

"*Jesus*, Ted."

"I know, right?"

Callie says, "She dumped you for another guy?"

He looks down. "Yeah."

"What about your kids? How are *they* taking it?"

"That's the worst part: they're thrilled. The new guy's younger, richer, cooler."

"How's that *possible*?" Callie says, with more than a hint of sarcasm.

"He's a pro basketball player."

She laughs, then apologizes. Then says, "But seriously: the guy's got it all. Including a bigger dick, I assume."

"Much bigger," Ted says. "According to Miriam."

"She said that to your *face*?"

"Yeah. Well, over the phone, if we're being technical."

Callie says, "What a bitch! It worked."

"What do you mean?"

"I *do* feel sorry for you. What's Miriam's last name?"

"Carstairs."

"Like car and stairs?"

"Yeah."

"I hate her." To me, she says, "Why do I want to cut Miriam's tits off and sew them in her mouth?"

"Because it's the right thing to do," I say.

Encouraged, Ted says, "Bottom line, besides my clothes and phone, this car's the only thing I got to keep after the divorce. It's my living. I literally can't live without it."

Taking him at his word, I crush his neck, lower the passenger seat, and pull him toward me, while backing out of the car. Callie helps me get him into the back seat, and together, we push him onto the floor and cover him with our luggage.

"I liked him," Callie said.

"Me too."

"I know he said he couldn't live without his car, but you were gonna kill him anyway, right?"

"Yes. But this way it was more like *his* decision."

"That's so *sweet*," she says.

When we get halfway to Vegas, five miles after the desert becomes vast, we pull off the road and find a suitable place to dump Ted's body.

PART 4

Punch & Judy

Chapter 1

FOR THREE DAYS, Punch and Judy have been sharing connecting rooms with a couple of killers whose names they don't know. The two rooms are in Punch and Judy's names, respectively. They checked in first, then gave the killers keys to both rooms. The killers shared a king bed, Punch and Judy did the same. When the killers left their room, Punch and Judy were required to stay in theirs, and the *Do Not Disturb* sign remained on the killers' door at all times.

When Punch and Judy first entered their rooms, Judy expressed her displeasure at the single king bed. If individual rooms were out of the question, she at least wanted two doubles. Punch pointed out their instructions had been strict: no exceptions. But Judy was adamant: if she didn't get a private room, she was out of there.

Fearing for Judy's life, Punch sat her down and told her about Amanda Lockmere, recently engaged, who'd been murdered before his very eyes three hours before he and Judy met. The skeptical Judy went straight to her laptop, punched in Amanda's name, and saw two things that gave her a better understanding of the people she'd gotten involved with: the first, a missing girl website featuring a recent photo of Amanda. The second, an article about how Amanda had gone missing from a hotel parking lot in Louisville, Kentucky on the same day Judy received the call from her contact, the guy who calls himself Robert.

She turned to Punch. “She looks like she could be my twin sister.”

“Brace yourself: the killer looks even more like you than Amanda did.”

“What about her partner?”

“We’re doppelgangers.”

“What’s that?”

“People who share the identical looks and general mannerisms of other people.”

“We look like murderers?”

“Yes. And we’re their alibis.”

“Are you saying they’re going to kill someone and we’re going to death row?”

“No. I mean, yeah, they’re probably going to kill someone, while posing as us. It’s possible we’ll be investigated, and possibly even arrested, but the cops won’t have any evidence that ties us to the crime because we’re normal people with normal jobs.”

Judy closes her eyes and shakes her head. “What the fuck have I done?”

“It’ll be okay.”

“How can you *say* that? You saw her kill Amanda! How could you not *tell* me that?”

“I didn’t want to scare you.”

“Oh, *really*? So instead, you allowed me to put my life in danger.”

“No offense, Judy, but you put your life in danger the minute you cashed your first paycheck, same as me and Amanda.”

“We’ve spent a hundred hours together since then. You could have warned me.”

“It wouldn’t have mattered. If you said no, like Amanda did, you’d have been dead within the hour.” He paused. “But the good news is, all we have to do is follow the script and we'll be fine. Robert gave me his word."

Judy said, "Do you even know Robert's last name?"

"No. Do you?"

"No. So I doubt we can trust any promises he made. Here's a more likely scenario: they're going to kill someone, make sure they're seen doing it, and then they're going to kill us, so we can take the blame."

"I don't think so. I honestly believe they're with Homeland Security." Noting Judy's skeptical look, Punch said, "Think about it. How long have they been paying you a fortune for doing nothing?"

"Four years."

He nodded. "They've been paying me for thirty-two months."

"What's your point?"

"My point is, if I hadn't seen Amanda and the killer, you'd be the most beautiful woman I've ever seen in my entire life. But so far, I've seen three of you, and apparently there are others. Not to mention the guys that look like me. What type of organization could possibly locate so many identical people and afford to pay them for years before giving them a job to do?"

"The government?"

"That's right. And don't forget what Robert said: they've also been paying people to do the phony consultant jobs for us for years."

"What's your point?"

"They're not going to kill us because they need us for the interviews after they do whatever they're here to do. And if we come through for them, they'll keep us on the payroll." He paused. "I don't know about you, but if these killers are protecting our country and paying me a fortune to take vacations with a gorgeous woman, I consider that a win-win."

After thinking it over, Judy decided she didn't have much choice but to follow the script and be a good asset. "You talked to Robert just now. What did he say to do today?"

"Wear the right clothes and be seen doing what lovebirds do on ski vacations."

"That's old news."

"Right. But today we also need to be back in our room no later than 6:00 p.m."

"Is that when the killers will be visible?"

"I assume so."

"Have you seen the guy that looks like you?"

"Not yet, but we're meeting them tonight."

"Are you scared?"

"Of *him*? Fuck yeah! The last time I saw the *lady*, I literally shit my pants."

"What time are they coming?"

"All I know is sometime after six. Which reminds me: when we get back to the room, help me remember to prop their door open with the latch, since they won't have a key."

"We'll probably see *her* at six, but not him."

Punch gives her a look. "How come?"

"That's supposed to be *my* room, right? She'll probably enter it a few minutes after six, knock on our connecting-room door, and get the keys. She'll get the extra key to *our* room, too."

"Why?"

"She'll take that one to the guy, and he'll enter *our* room from now on to get to *their* room."

"Wow. You're good at this."

"So are you, but we need to get great. Tell me again what they want from us."

"Outside the room, we're lovebirds, on a week-long ski trip. We're supposed to post tons of photos on social media, send texts to our friends and relatives, answer their texts and emails, and do the stuff normal couples would do."

"Are you not totally creeped out that this killer who looks like you will be coming in and out of our room constantly?"

"I haven't really thought about it. But yeah, now that you mention it—"

"Did Robert give you any indication how long they're going to be here?"

"The killers?"

"Yeah, but let's call them something else."

"Good point. Like what?"

"Smith and Jones."

"Which is which?"

"She's Smith, he's Jones."

"I like it. So anyway, Robert said Smith and Jones will be here anywhere from a few hours to a few days, but we're staying the full week, regardless. And you're not supposed to shave your legs, underarms, or cooch until they leave."

"*Cooch?*"

Embarrassed, Punch shrugged. "I didn't know what to call it."

"What did *he* call it?"

"Your pussy."

Judy frowned. "Charming. Why?"

"I guess he wanted to be clear."

Judy shook her head. "I meant why am I not allowed to shave till they leave?"

"Because of the drains."

"What are you *talking* about?"

"The minute they leave, we need to move all your clothes and luggage into their room as fast as possible, and you need to turn on the lights and television and set out all your toiletries as if you've been using that room since the moment we arrived. And immediately after doing that, you need to brush your teeth, take a shower with a new bar of soap, and shave every part of your body you can."

"Why?"

"Because anything you forgot to lay out, you'll remember when taking a shower, or shaving, or getting dressed afterward. And because before they turn the room over to you, Smith and Jones are going to remove all their luggage, fingerprints, the soap and other personal items, and they're going to put something down the drains to get rid of their hair and any other DNA. If your DNA isn't on the soap and your fingerprints aren't all over the room, and your body hair isn't in the drain, it'll be hard to prove you've been using that room the whole time."

"Holy shit!"

"Like I said, these people are pros."

Chapter 2

AN HOUR AGO, as the fire alarm blared, Punch and Judy followed the guests down the steps, through the lobby, and outdoors to the parking lot. The Secret Service agents were rushing back and forth, shouting into walkie-talkies, making sure the hotel security guards were keeping the guests off the road. Within seconds, members of the Compton family were ushered quickly into waiting cars and whisked away.

"Where's Analise?" an elderly lady shouted.

Punch turned instinctively. Noticing the old lady was wearing only a nightgown and house slippers, he gallantly offered his jacket. At first, she refused, but Punch insisted, and when she finally accepted it she offered him God's blessing. Judy moved in for a kiss, and Punch gave her one. An hour later, they were back in Punch's hotel room, being questioned by the FBI.

Chapter 3

AFTER GIVING THEIR names and showing their driver's licenses, Punch and Judy answer all the FBI agents' questions. When asked if either of them had seen Analise Compton, Judy says she followed Analise into the bathroom for an autograph.

"When was this?"

She tells them.

"Did she sign something for you?"

"Yes, Sir."

"Do you still have it?"

"Of course." Judy digs it out of her handbag and shows it to them.

"May we have it?" they ask.

Judy balks. It pains her, but...sure. If they think it'll help in some way.

They ask a number of questions about Judy's moment with Analise in the rest room. "Was it just the two of you?"

"Yes."

"What was her demeanor?"

"Normal."

"Was she still there when you left?"

"Yes."

"What was she doing?"

"Entering one of the stalls."

"Did she say anything?"

"Not really."

The guy asking the questions gives her a skeptical look.

Judy says, "I mean, she asked if my boobs were real."

Punch tries not to roll his eyes.

"Your boobs?" the agent says.

"Yes, Sir."

"Why would she ask that?"

"I guess she was a little self-conscious about hers."

"What do you mean?"

"It was just girl talk. When I walked into the rest room I told her I was a huge fan, and asked for an autograph. She was really sweet. 'Of course,' she said. She used her own pen. I told her she was even prettier in person than on TV. She said, 'You really think so?' I said, 'Absolutely.' She said she was a bit self-conscious about her boobs, and asked if I could tell they were fake. I could, but pretended I couldn't. You know, just to be nice. She asked if mine were real, and I laughed and said, 'They're way too small to be fake.'"

The agents instinctively glance at Judy's chest, then ask if she and Punch know anyone in Park City.

They don't.

The agent tries again: "Ever heard of a woman named Alma Swingbee? She's a little person."

"A midget," the other one says. "Runs a boarding house in Park City."

"Nope. Sorry," Punch says.

Judy says, "Wait: is she the tiny lady we met at the hotel yesterday?"

Punch says, "You're right! We met a little person, a woman, but very briefly. We didn't exchange much information."

"Did she say why she was here?"

"She told us she worked here, part-time."

"Doing what?"

"Event coordinating."

They change the subject. "Have you been watching the local news?"

Judy grins. "To be honest, we've been consumed with having sex."

They look at her as if picturing what it would be like. Then one of them says, "Were you aware one of her boarders was murdered several days ago?"

Judy looks at Punch quizzically. "What's a boarder?"

"A person who rents a room."

Punch and Judy had no idea.

"It gets worse," the agent says. "The two detectives that were investigating the murder were killed just hours after speaking to Ms. Swingbee."

"You think she killed them?"

"We're not sure. But it could have been another one of her boarders. A guy named Jonathan Cablemoor. All we know about him is he's missing, and he used to be president of his homeowner's association."

Punch and Judy tell the agents they've never been to Park City and don't know anything about Mrs. Swingbee or her boarders.

After another half-hour of questions, the agents leave.

"That's *it*?" Judy says. "I plastered the room with fingerprints, used the soap, shaved my cooch, and they barely even checked it!"

Punch grins. "Shaved your what?"

She shrugs. "I don't like saying pussy."

"What do you call it?"

"I'm not telling you."

"I like what you said about how we've been consumed with having sex."

"Oh really? Well, don't get any ideas," she says.

"All I have is ideas."

PART 5

Callie, Creed, & Analise

Chapter 1

NORMALLY WE DON'T burn our operatives, but Alma gave us no choice. The fact she'd been having an affair with my first Park City victim, the Preacher, didn't bother me. But what the Preacher said before dying bothered me a lot. He said I'd never get away with it because Alma told him all about me and the jobs she'd done for us in the past. Which reminded me, once again, no one can be trusted.

Alma knew the rules: if you talk, you die. As for the others, obviously Callie and I had to kill everyone that saw us at the boarding house, including the detectives and Jonathan Cablemoor, the former president of his neighborhood homeowner's association. Collateral damage is always as unpleasant as it is necessary, and we work hard to minimize it. For this reason, we didn't kill the rest of Alma's boarders. We're trusting if anyone else happened to see us they'll be too frightened to report it.

In the meantime, Callie and I are driving to Las Vegas, where she owns a multi-million-dollar penthouse condo. At the moment, she's behind the wheel. Since I'm not the least bit tired, I pepper her with questions about how she managed the abduction.

At first, she plays it coy: "I hypnotized her and the Secret Service guy. Then I commanded him to look the other way while I made her follow me to Alma's car."

"You've already spilled the part Judy played in distracting the agent. Tell me what really happened."

"Fine. I was in the skating area, checking out the stuff they had on sale. While Randy put on his skates, Analise helped the kids. She hugged Randy and sent them off to the skating rink, and two of the agents went with them, leaving just one to guard Analise. She wanted to use the bathroom, so the Secret Service guy cleared it for her and guarded the door. Moments later, a lady needed to use the bathroom, and the agent wouldn't let her. But Analise heard them arguing, and told him to stop being a jerk. She made him stand by the skate counter, which was about thirty feet away. By then the lady had stormed off in a huff, so I entered the restroom, put Analise in a choke hold, and called Judy. After making sure she was wearing the same clothes as me, I told her to come to the skate shop and distract the Secret Service guy while I carried Analise to Alma's car over my shoulder." She looks at me and smiles. "And that's the whole story. I swear."

"Is any part of that bullshit story true?" I ask.

"Yes."

"Which part?"

"Which part do you think?"

"How far is the skate shop from the parking garage?"

"Four hundred yards, give or take."

"A quarter mile," I say, thinking it over.

"That's right."

"In that case I believe everything you said until you got inside the bathroom."

"You don't believe I put her in a choke hold?"

"No."

"Why not?"

"Four reasons: one, you somehow got Analise to give you an autograph, which you somehow gave to Judy. Two, you couldn't carry the president's daughter over your shoulder all the way from the skate shop to Alma's car without being seen. Three, Punch and Judy didn't know why the alarms went off in the hotel afterward, so she didn't distract the agent while you and Analise were still in the bathroom. If she had, she would have seen you and therefore would have known you kidnapped Analise."

"Did you just say 'Therefore?'"

"I did."

"What's the fourth reason you don't believe me?"

"The Secret Service agent was watching the bathroom from the skate counter, which means he saw you enter the bathroom. If Judy had showed up to distract him before you walked out, he would have known something was up. After all, she looks exactly like you and was wearing the exact same clothes."

"Unless she was wearing her granny panties."

"I stand corrected," I say. "But since he wouldn't have *seen* her panties, he would've assumed she was you. So, what really happened?"

"You tell me. And if you guess right, I'll confirm."

"If I get it right, it won't be a guess. It'll be the result of carefully-constructed deductions based on precise calculations, utilizing the principles of logic, reason, science, and human nature."

"Donovan?"

"Yeah?"

"Just see if you can figure it out."

"You promise you'll confirm?"

"I promise."

Lying is such an essential part of our business, Callie and I often hone our skills by purposely lying to each other. When she says, "I swear,"—as she did earlier—she may or may not be telling the truth. And if she tells you or someone else "I promise," she might very well be lying. But when she tells *me* "I promise", well, that's the real deal. So, I think it over to see if I can determine what really happened in the ski shop bathroom, and after a couple of minutes, this is what I come up with:

"Analise was in on it."

"What do you mean?"

"She knew about the kidnapping in advance. The general—or someone else who had knowledge of the kidnapping—showed Analise our photos and briefed her about us. When she saw you lurking in the ski shop she recognized you and waited for you to follow her into the restroom. Am I right?"

"Yes. But that's the easy part. How did we get out of the bathroom without being seen?"

"You left first, and she stayed behind. You went to the parking garage, got in Alma's car, left Analise's autograph on the front seat. Then you popped the trunk so Analise would know where to go."

"Well done. But how did she get out of the bathroom without being seen?"

"Before leaving the bathroom you called Judy and made sure she was wearing the same clothes. But you didn't tell her to go directly to the skate shop. You told her to go to the parking garage first, get the autograph, and *then* go to the skate shop. That way the agent would see Judy coming back from the direction you left and think she was you. He'd naturally be interested in any comment Judy might make, and therefore it was easy for her to distract him."

"Excellent. Exactly right. But stop saying 'therefore.' It's really pissing me off. What are you doing?"

"Patting myself on the back."

"It looks ridiculous."

"You didn't say that in the old days after we had sex."

"No, but I was *thinking* it. And anyway, your back pats are like your ejaculations: premature."

I frown.

She says, "I'm saying that because you haven't answered the key question: Analise is world-famous, and the hotel was filled to bursting with holiday guests, so how did she get out of the bathroom without *Judy* seeing her, and how did she walk 400 yards from the ski shop to the parking garage without being recognized by anyone else?"

I start to say something, then change my mind. "I have no clue. Tell me."

"You give up?"

"Yes."

"Say it."

"I give up."

When she starts patting herself on the back I say, "You're right. It *does* look ridiculous."

"Only when *you* do it," she says.

"Are you going to tell me or not?"

"Not."

"Fuck you!"

"Sorry," she says. "But that ship has sailed."

Chapter 2

NOW, IN CALLIE'S penthouse, she pours us a drink and starts playing what she calls "music" while we wait on Anson, who's several hours behind us. That's because after leaving us by the bridge near Park City, he had to drive his rental car to the abandoned farm outside Provo where our windowless van has been sitting in a barn for the past three weeks. Then he had to wait for Analise to wake up, pee, stretch her legs, and then he fed her, gave her plenty of water, and put her in the trunk in the back of the van. Before closing the lid, he gave her another sedative.

After twenty minutes of Callie's angry rap tunes, she can tell I'm fed up. "Let me guess," she says. "You'd rather hear codger music?"

"If I said yes, what would you play?"

"I only have the CDs you gave me years ago, for my birthday."

"Any of those would be wonderful."

I watch her remove the cellophane from one of the CDs. "You never bothered to open them?"

"No offense, but that shit puts me to sleep."

"How do you know?"

"Educated guess."

"Well, it'll do you good to hear some real music."

"What's your definition of *that*?"

"Real music? Simple. It's anything that doesn't destroy your eardrums or melt your brain cells."

"Good to know. Who's this guy?"

"Excuse me?"

She holds up the CD. "Sam Cooke. Who's he?"

I lift my head, close my eyes, take a deep breath. Then open my eyes and say, "You're joking, right?"

She shrugs, puts it in her CD player.

While she does that I say, "Sam Cooke had the sweetest voice in all the world."

She rolls her eyes.

I say, "Play track number six. *Unchained Melody*. It'll change your life."

She laughs, presses a button, and as Sam sings...all the stress in the world melts from my body. Afterward, I look up, expecting to catch her sneering at me, but see only tears spilling from her eyes.

I smile. "It's great, isn't it!"

"It's okay."

"You seemed moved just now."

"I was moved by how it affected *you*. I wish I loved music the way you do."

"You might, if you give it a try."

"I just did."

We compromise by finishing our drinks, and pouring another.

"Any updates from the general?" she asks.

"No."

"We could have killed her ten times already, but we didn't. How come?"

"Leverage."

"What do you mean?"

I take a few minutes to explain my desperate financial situation. Naturally, she thinks I'm an idiot for giving Trudy twenty million. But she's more interested in my motive: "You think the general had something to do with stealing your money?"

"I'm sure of it."

"You're going to keep her alive till he gives it back?"

"If I can."

"This should be interesting."

Around 4 a.m., Anson calls to say he's making a delivery. As we head to the private parking garage, Callie gives him the gate code. Anson punches it into the keypad, enters the parking garage, parks the van, and helps us unload the trunk onto the cargo dolly, where I use a heat-detecting wand to perform a quick scan of the contents. Anson knows better than to question if I trust him. He knows I can't afford to trust anyone. Satisfied the trunk contains a live human, I thank him for all he's done.

"Get some sleep," I say, knowing full well he won't.

He nods, climbs back in the van, and we watch him drive away.

"He's good," Callie says.

"The best."

"Did you think he put a bomb inside her?"

"No."

"Then why'd you use a bomb-detector wand just now?"

I smile. "You noticed that?"

"How could I not?"

"You think Anson noticed?"

"No. But it doesn't matter. I think he knows not to fuck with us."

She slings Analise's oversized hand bag over her shoulder and holds the door for me as I tilt the trunk onto the dolly and push it toward the elevator. When we get to the penthouse, I wheel the trunk into Callie's third bedroom, and she and I lower it to the floor, open it up, and check out the contents.

"What do you think?" Callie says.

"She's stunning," I say.

"I agree," Callie says. "Can I keep her?"

Chapter 3

SINCE ANALISE IS still unconscious, Callie and I lift her out of the trunk, place her on the guest bed, and take turns guarding her. After sleeping an hour, I grab my laptop, swing by the kitchen and retrieve a bottle of water from Callie's fridge, then head to the second guestroom and tap lightly on the door.

Callie tells me to come in.

"How is she?" I ask.

"Anson must've given her the full dose," Callie says. "She's still out."

I notice Callie's TV is covering the story. "Do they have any leads?"

"They found a rifle typically used by the North Koreans, but there were no prints on it. The rifle was used to shoot a Secret Service agent, but they're not sure why, since Analise was nowhere near the agent at the time of the shooting."

"That *does* sound mysterious. What's the official designation: missing or kidnapped?"

"Missing. But they're convinced she's been kidnapped."

"Have any groups come forward to take credit?"

"Nope. Nor have any demands been made."

"Any conspiracy theories?"

"Tons! They were smart to include the assault rifle. Makes it hard for either political party to blame the other."

"Is it bringing the Senate and Congress together?"

"Totally! No one's talking about the issues. They're all showing genuine support."

"How big a story is it?"

"It's all they're showing, and it's just getting started. They expect more than 60% of the country to miss work today."

"Why?"

"They'll be glued to TV and social media."

"Amazing!"

I turn my attention to Analise, who's exactly as I left her, with two exceptions: she's currently barefoot...and she's wearing one of our ankle bracelets. "Have you activated it?"

"No. I think she deserves a warning. Plus, I'd like to avoid the noise and mess, if possible."

I power up my laptop, aim it at Analise, then ask Callie if she wants a copy.

"Nope. I've scanned her twice already."

I laugh. "I'm sure you have!"

I check Analise's eyelids and pulse. "She seems fine. You should get some rest. I'll take over."

"Sounds good. But call me if she wakes up, okay?"

I nod.

Callie asks if there's anything I need.

"Nope. I'm good."

"In that case, I'll see you in an hour."

The hour comes and goes, and when Callie enters the room I head back to my guest room to rest. An hour later I rise, piss, brush my teeth, wash my face and hands, then go to Analise's room, where

I find both ladies sitting across from each other, drinking coffee. Analise is on the bed, Callie's in the comfy chair. When Callie formally introduces me to Analise Compton I ask, "How are you feeling?"

"Disappointed."

Callie says, "Analise feels she's not being treated properly."

"Specifically," Analise says, "I don't appreciate being drugged and stuffed into a luggage trunk. I'm banged up and bruised, and none of it was necessary."

"Why's that?"

"I came with Miss Carpenter voluntarily."

"So?"

"I understand why she had to keep me in the trunk of the car for a short period. But I climbed in of my own volition, so there was no need to inject dangerous drugs into my system. After driving a short distance, Ms. Carpenter should have released me from the trunk and allowed me to ride in the car as a passenger. I obviously wouldn't have caused any trouble, since my presence was the result of a voluntary action."

I pause. "Do you always talk like that?"

"Like what?"

I shake my head. "Never mind. Look, I know you're accustomed to the finer things in life, but we're simple kidnappers. This is how we operate, meaning, we're not accustomed to taking chances."

"You may be kidnappers, but it's a well-known fact your expertise is murder. Nevertheless, I offered my participation without a hint of resistance, to show good faith. And I feel it's not been reciprocated."

"I suppose we could kill you."

"No, you can't."

"Why not?"

"It's not part of our bargain."

I look at Callie for the second time. She explains, "Analise believes you and the general have an agreement that she's to be our guest for an unspecified time, during which she is to be treated with the utmost care and respect." She smiles. "Speaking of which, she wants a pen and some paper so she can write a list of the things she requires to make her time here as comfortable as possible."

"Like what?" I ask. "Brioche to feed the pigeons?"

Callie says, "We don't have pigeons in Las Vegas."

"Yeah, you do. But you call them gamblers."

Analise says, "I'm not asking for the moon. Just a few basic items and simple courtesies."

"Such as?"

"My phone. A computer with wi-fi. An assortment of clothes. Some specialty food items, if you don't already have them in your fridge or pantry. Some personal hygiene products, including a particular brand of European soap and shampoo and a specific European laundry detergent for when I wash my clothes. And obviously, the freedom to move around the residence, including access to the kitchen. If that sounds reasonable, I won't be any trouble. You'll hardly notice I'm here."

"Anything else?"

"At the moment, no. I'm ready to watch your video."

Callie says, "She's talking about the ankle bracelet video."

I nod. "Good idea. I think you'll find it enlightening. Would you like us to prepare some popcorn for the viewing?"

Analise frowns. "You needn't be sarcastic, Mr. Creed. The few things I'm asking for are basic human necessities that fall within the bounds of common decency. They're far less than I'd offer you if you were *my* houseguest."

"Obviously your phone's out of the question, since the FBI has already set up a task force to search for the signal. But why can't you use domestic soap, shampoo, or laundry products?"

Analise goes into lecture mode: "Do you have any idea how many dangerous chemicals the U.S. Food and Drug Administration prohibits from these types of products?"

"This might shock you, but no."

"Eleven, including mercury and chloroform."

"If they prohibit those chemicals, what's the problem?"

"The European Union prohibits more than 1,300."

"You're saying European personal products are safe."

"Not at all. European companies use more than 12,000 chemicals in their products, ninety percent of which have never been tested for safety. So, no, they're not safe. They're just a lot safer than ours."

"Thanks for the information."

"If you eat the food and use the products I request, you'll both be healthier for it."

"Will hotdogs be on your list?"

Analise says nothing, but her look of disdain tells me she doesn't suffer smart asses. I get us back on track: "Let's discuss your ankle bracelet."

"Let's do."

"I'm sure you've seen or at least heard about the ankle bracelets your father's friends have to wear when they're under house arrest for banking fraud and other types of white collar crimes." When she fails to respond I say, "*Have* you seen or heard of those?"

"Yes," she says. "We call them ankle monitors. They emit a constant radio frequency signal that tells law enforcement where the person is at all times."

"That's correct. But this one's different."

"How so?"

Chapter 4

"THE BRACELET ON your ankle isn't a location monitor. It's more like a bomb."

She stares at it a moment. "I don't believe you."

"When Callie activates it, you'll be confined to this room, and the adjoining bathroom. If you attempt to exit this area the bracelet will explode. It won't blow up the entire building, but it will certainly separate your foot from your leg, and you'll likely suffer severe burns all the way up to—and possibly including—your lower abdomen."

"Look: you don't need to make up fantastic stories. I'm not planning to cause any trouble. But I do expect the freedom to move through the house."

"We knew you wouldn't believe us about the bracelet, but perhaps you'll trust the video."

Callie presses the start arrow on the screen, and hands it to Analise.

The video begins with a closeup of an identical ankle bracelet being placed on the ankle of a man who appears to be in an interrogation room. After securing the bracelet, a voice tells the man he's free to go. The man hesitates a moment, then walks through the open door, and a loud explosion, followed by blood-curdling screams, can be heard. The man is carried back into the room, and the camera records his significant, life-threatening injuries.

"The good news," Callie says, "the man survived, though they did have to amputate his leg." She smiles. "You have world-class legs, Analise. Please don't lose one of them."

The expression of horror remains frozen on Analise's face long after the video ends. Eventually she looks up at me and says, "Either I've been lied to, or you're reneging on your end of the deal. Which is it?"

"You've been lied to."

"I see. May I inquire about your intentions?"

"We're sort of playing it by ear."

"What does that mean?"

"In a perfect world you'd be dead by now."

She looks at me with great concern. "*That's* your idea of a perfect world?"

I smile. "No offense. As you so aptly pointed out, we're killers, not kidnappers, so we expect to make some mistakes along the way. And the longer we *keep* you here the more mistakes we're likely to make. So, we've decided to restrict your movements for the time being."

"You can't possibly be afraid of me."

"We're concerned about your knowledge of the kidnapping."

"Well, of *course* I knew! They needed my permission." She takes a breath. "Look, I appreciate not being dead right now, but it's obvious I have my own people to thank for that, not you. I was told you were wealthy, and a major contributor to my father's campaign. I was assured you had a lot to gain by participating in this endeavor, and that you'd treat me graciously, and with full resect. I was promised I wouldn't be tied up, abused, drugged, and that I'd have freedom of movement, and wouldn't lack for creature comforts, which is why it appears to me that *you're* the ones reneging on the deal."

"Why do you suppose they hired killers to kidnap you?"

"I assume it's because they trust you, having worked with you in Homeland Security. But here's a better question: why did they want me kidnapped in the first place?"

"That's the obvious part. Your father's been under siege since day one of his presidency. He's been crucified nonstop by the press, and his approval rating is off a cliff. He's despised by a high percentage of Americans, his own political party is publicly criticizing him for his ties to organized crime, and he's facing criminal charges for bribery, tax evasion, and money laundering. Congress is in total gridlock, and your father can't get any portion of his agenda advanced."

"That's all common knowledge. What's your point?"

"Being a military man, I think his chief advisor, General Barry, wanted to create a diversion. Something that would take the heat off your father, create unity, and position him as a sympathetic character. So, he concocted a scheme to have you kidnapped. Am I right?"

"Not exactly, but why do you suppose *I* was chosen?"

"Lots of reasons: you're an only child, you're bright, amazingly popular, and most important, you're beautiful. The general knows there's nothing more tantalizing to the press than the kidnapping of a beautiful girl. And the fact you're the president's daughter guarantees this will be the biggest story of the century. Your parents are, of course, grief-stricken. But since you're not identified with your father's politics, you won't be judged by his policies. So, your kidnapping makes a great deal of sense. What I don't understand is why the general let you in on it?"

"Maybe he was afraid I'd get hurt if I resisted."

"That's one possibility."

"The general told me all about you and Ms. Carpenter and said I should play along, remain quiet, and you'd take me to your estate, which is secure, well-fortified, and nicer than any country club in America. They said I'd be wined and dined, and provided with every manner of comforts."

"And did they explain when you'd be rescued? And how?"

"Yes, of course. But that part's mostly up to me. I'll follow the narrative, and when the time is right, I'll make a phone call."

"To whom?"

"I've memorized the names and phone numbers of two women, either of whom can help coordinate the extraction, with your help."

"Who are they?"

She pauses. "I think it's to my advantage not to reveal them at this time."

"Well, if I'm supposed to work with them the general must have reason to believe I would."

She nods.

"Can you tell me what business they're in?"

Analise purses her lips. "I think they're professionals." When I fail to react, she clarifies: "Prostitutes."

Callie laughs. "Of course, they are!"

I get us back on track: "What did you mean when you said you'd follow the narrative?"

"To be specific, I'm referring to the news cycle. How long has it been since I was kidnapped?"

"About eight hours."

She nods. "We believe the kidnapping will dominate the current news cycle for 48 hours because that time span is considered critical. We're counting on the media to hammer that point home, and if they do, we believe people will watch day and night for updates. Despite what *you* think, my father has millions of extremely devoted supporters, whom we expect to go crazy. Conspiracy theories should dominate conservative radio, TV, and social media platforms, and the liberal stations will run features on me and the special relationship I have with my father. All the coverage is expected to be positive for my father."

"Is that why you agreed to the kidnapping?"

"I'm in it because I love my father, and believe his policies have a right to be tested."

"Do *you* believe in his policies?"

"Not all of them. But I believe in *him*."

"Did the general come up with a code name for this operation?"

Analise almost smiles. "How'd you know?"

"I worked with him for years. The man can't take a dump without giving it a code name. What's this one called?"

"Operation HTP."

"Which means?"

"Humanize the president."

Callie laughs.

I ask, "What was supposed to happen after the initial 48 hours of news coverage?"

"We figured the media would run hot and heavy for three or four days before running out of coverage angles and people to interview. As the story dies down, a steady trickle of credible information will be released."

"Like what?"

"Messages and demands from the kidnappers. Not *you* guys, of course, since that would be too risky. They'll use others who are in on it."

With great annoyance, Callie asks, "How many people know what's going on?"

"Six, possibly seven."

"I don't like it."

"You needn't worry. They're 100% loyal to my father."

"No one's that loyal. If they're caught, they'll talk."

I say, "How do they plan to make demands? Without photos or voice recordings, there's no way to prove you're alive."

Analise smiles. "We made recordings last week. Staged, with an old-timey cassette tape recorder. No way to trace them. They'll be released in a specific progression from different parts of the country. It's a very sophisticated plan."

"What do *you* think would have happened if you'd said no to the kidnapping?"

"They would've called it off."

"I don't think so," Callie says.

"I can guarantee it," Analise says.

"I'm listening."

"The kidnapping wasn't the general's idea."

Callie arches a perfect eyebrow. "Whose idea was it?"

"Whose do you think?"

"Your father's?" Callie says.

"Your husband's?" I say.

"You're both wrong," Analise says. "It was *my* idea."

I study her face. "Then why were my orders to kidnap you and kill you as quickly as possible?"

Analise says, "Those *weren't* your orders, and the proof is right in front of you: I'm still alive."

"For now."

She frowns. "I remain quite disappointed by your attitude. This is a business arrangement, nothing more. My side negotiated in good faith, and here you are, after the fact, making threats and treating me poorly. There's obviously been a misunderstanding, and I think if you'll call the general he'll clear it up."

"Are you positive your husband doesn't want you dead?"

"Why would that idea even cross your mind?"

"Because if this was *your* idea, you would have discussed it with Randy, who works directly with General Barry in the White House. What I'm saying, Randy would have worked out all the details with the general."

"Randy and I have a wonderful relationship. He would never want me dead."

"So you're saying it was General Barry's decision? Why would *he* want you dead?"

Chapter 5

"I DON'T BELIEVE the general or anyone else wants me dead," Analise says. "That would destroy all the good will we're trying to build."

Callie says, "Maybe he's afraid she'll screw up the extraction, or the FBI interrogations after she's rescued."

"Or maybe it's something far more sinister," I say.

"Like what?"

"He wanted us to shoot an agent with a North Korean weapon. If he could pin her death on the North Koreans, it might rally the public and give him an excuse to start a war."

Analise says, "You *shot* someone? I was told no one would get hurt."

"You never heard mention of a North Korean rifle being used?"

"Not used, but left at the scene to fuel conspiracy theories."

"*That* sounds like your father's White House!"

"Mr. Creed?"

"Yeah?"

"Did you in fact contribute millions to my father's campaign?"

"No."

"Then why was I told that?"

"To make you feel comfortable, I suppose."

She takes a moment before saying, "I want to know what *you* think about my father."

"No, you don't."

"Please."

Chapter 6

"THIS ISN'T ABOUT your father specifically," I say. "I don't like *any* politicians."

"My father's not a politician," Analise says. "If nothing else, the election proved it! The voters *hate* Congress. They wanted someone with zero political experience."

"That can't be true."

"Just because *you* don't support my father doesn't mean—"

"Analise, I don't give a rat's ass who the president is, provided I get funding to do my job. All I meant was I don't believe anyone would vote for a candidate simply because he has no experience. It's like saying people who hate doctors would hire a plumber to perform their surgeries."

She frowns. "It's not the same thing."

"Isn't it?"

"No. People wanted a change. So, they elected my father."

"And how's that working out?"

"As of this morning, quite well."

"Unless we kill you."

She looks up at me through impossibly large, pretty eyes and says, "But you're *not* going to kill me, correct?"

"Not today."

"Does that mean you'll consider my list?"

"Don't press your luck. Can I ask *you* a question?"

Analise nods.

"Why did you touch your bra just now?"

"What do you mean?"

Callie says, "It's the first thing you did after regaining consciousness, too. You touched the fabric between your bra cups."

I add, "You've done it twice since I entered the room. I'm simply asking why you did that."

"I'm...not aware I did. I'm sure it was involuntary."

"I don't think so. I think you're wearing a tracking device."

"What are you *talking* about?"

"Being kidnapped is dangerous as hell. I think someone—probably Randy—was concerned something might go wrong. It strikes me you might have some sort of tracking device in your bra."

"That's crazy."

"So, it's not true?"

"Of course not."

I study her face a moment, then say, "I believe you."

"Thank you."

"And yet, you're lying."

"Why would you *say* that?"

"We've scanned you several times."

"Scanned me how?"

"With our computers."

"What are you *talking* about?"

I give her a lecture of my own: "On January 7, 2010, President Obama authorized the use of full body scanners in airports that were so effective they could reveal people's genitals. But with a simple click of a button, the photos could be inverted to show every graphic detail in vivid color. In other words, before inversion, they could tell which way my penis was hanging. But after inversion, they could literally see the dorsal vein on my penis. When the public learned how invasive these scanners were, they went nuts. Apart from personal privacy issues, the scanners violated child pornography laws. So, changes were made, and now the scanners are far less invasive. But just because the original ones are no longer being used in airports doesn't mean the technology was abandoned."

"What do you mean?" she says, nervously.

"Our computers are equipped with those original scanners. Shortly after drugging you, Callie performed a scan of your body. And we scanned you again, while you were unconscious. Every inch of your body is visible on our computers."

She glances at my computer. "I don't believe you."

I open my computer, access the program, and aim the built-in camera at her. "Women's breasts are never perfectly symmetrical. Typically, the left breast is slightly larger than the right, and the size differential ranges from slight to 20%."

"Why are you telling me this?"

"Because in your case, even though you have implants, your right breast is slightly larger. Also, in the first scan, your left nipple was erect. Now, they're both erect."

She stands. "If I believed for one minute you have an actual scan of my naked body on your computer, I'd sue the shit out of you."

I turn the computer screen toward her and say, "The tracking device is clearly visible under your bra, between your breasts. Please remove it and hand it to me."

She stares at the picture. Her eyes bug out. She gasps, "You motherfucker!"

"Relax, Analise. You're moments away from getting a pen and paper."

"*Relax*? Are you *shitting* me? You've got a nude photo of me on your computer! That's a felony! You're going to do prison time for this!"

"If I do, you won't live to see it. Remove your bra and hand it to me."

She takes two steps toward me and slaps my face as hard as she can. Obviously, I saw it coming from a mile away and could have easily avoided it, but I wanted to feel how hard she hits.

She didn't disappoint!

I suddenly love that about her, and hope she'll hit me again, with her left hand, but she restrains herself and surprises me by saying, "I'm sorry. I've never hit anyone like that before."

"It's okay. Did you enjoy it?"

"No. I hate to lose control of my emotions. Please don't tell anyone I did that."

"Your secret's safe with us. Now, if you don't mind, please remove your bra."

She stares at me a moment, then says, "Do you intend to just stand there and watch?"

"I was hoping to."

Callie holds up a small piece of black metal and says, "He's just messing with you. I removed it and crushed it before we ever left the parking garage."

It takes Analise a moment to realize the enormity of what's happened. Until this moment she thought Randy and General Barry knew her precise location. Now she realizes she's completely cut off from the people she was counting on to protect her.

She starts crying.

I motion Callie to follow me out of the room. Before doing so, Callie reminds Analise that her safe zone is limited to this bedroom, bathroom, and closet.

Now, in the kitchen, I tell Callie, "I think we've got a problem."

"Are you talking about how she's supposed to call the hookers when she's ready to go home?"

"Partly. But mostly I'm talking about how the general told her about my estate."

"What's the problem? We're here, not there."

"The problem is, Randy knows the tracking device stopped working. He's got to be worried sick about his wife."

"Worried enough to tell the FBI there may have been two sets of us at the hotel?"

"Possibly. But even if he doesn't, if Analise fails to contact the hookers within a reasonable amount of time, I expect he'll tell the FBI what he knows. If that happens, they'll raid my place first, then yours, looking for her. If we're not at our respective homes when that happens, they'll suspect we're with her. And that's a problem."

"I agree," Callie says. "But let's not forget we've also got three loose ends."

"Three? Punch, Judy, and who else?"

"Anson."

"Anson isn't a loose end."

"He will be if the FBI comes calling."

"I disagree. He's in it up to his neck."

"They'll give him immunity."

"For his role in the kidnapping? Certainly. But not for all the other shit I've got on him."

"For now, I'll trust your judgment. But what about Punch and Judy?"

I remove my burner phone from my back pocket. "Watch and learn."

Chapter 7

WHEN PUNCH ANSWERS, I put the phone on speaker and say, "How's it going?"

"The hotel's swarming with reporters and news crews. They're interviewing every guest and employee they can find."

"But not you and Judy."

"No. We refused to talk to them."

"How did you phrase that?"

"We told them we're too scared."

"Perfect. The reason I'm calling, we have reason to believe the FBI might try to remove you and Judy from the premises to question you in a secret facility."

Callie rolls her eyes.

Punch says, "Why would they suspect *us*?"

"They know Judy was the last person that saw her. They think you guys have more information than you're sharing."

"Shit! What should we do?"

"Wait for us to come get you, but that'll take at least six hours. In the meantime, I want you each to swallow one of the large pills Robert gave you."

"The silver ones?"

"Yes."

"What good will that do?"

"The pills contain a built-in tracking device. If you each take one now, they'll stay in your body for at least two days. If the FBI takes you before we get there, we'll be able to locate you."

"Why do *both* of us need to take the pills?"

"Because if they remove you from the premises, they'll split you up. We can't save you if you don't take the pills."

"Got it. Want us to do it right now?"

"Yes."

We hear him tell Judy to take one of the large silver pills. She asks why, and he tells her the whole story. Callie whispers, "They're so sweet! I'm gonna miss them."

"Me too."

A moment goes by while they locate their respective pills. "Okay," he says. "We're good."

"Great. But don't hang up just yet. Callie wants to say something. She's in the next room. Give me just a minute."

"Of course."

I wait till I hear them gagging and choking. When they start vomiting, I hang up.

Callie asks, "Why didn't you just give them the regular death pills?"

"Too small. The pills had to be huge, or they wouldn't have believed they contained a tracking device."

"But they weren't metal, were they?"

"No, but Punch and Judy wouldn't know they have to be metal."

"Cool," Callie says. "I'll make you a deal: if you make us some breakfast, I'll destroy your burner phone."

I hand her the phone. "Deal!"

"I'd also like to give Analise a pen and paper."

"Why?"

"I want to find out what products she uses."

"Are you actually thinking about buying them for her?"

She shrugs. "Maybe after breakfast." She pauses, then says, "Are you okay?"

"Huh?"

"You're staring into space."

"Oh. Sorry. I'm just trying to figure out where we can stash her. We can't keep her here, and we can't take her to any property associated with us."

"We'll also need to get someone to watch her while we demonstrate we're living at our respective homes."

"You have someone in mind?"

"No one I'd trust to guard the president's daughter! How about you?"

"Only Anson. But he needs to stay at my place."

We're quiet, lost in thought, till Callie asks, "What about your Ultimate Favors? Is anyone dumb enough to have granted you one?"

I grin. "Holy shit! You're a genius! Yes!"

"Anyone I know?"

"As a matter of fact, yes."

"Tell me."

"Dani Ripper."

Chapter 8

"*WHAT?* YOU CAN'T be serious! *Dani?*"

"Yup."

"Why would she agree to *that?*"

"I helped her with a case last year."

"Must've been a helluva case!"

"It was. I got her a name and address from WitSec."

"Bullshit! No one's *ever* broken into Witness Protection."

"*I* did. Obviously, they don't advertise it."

She laughs. "I was only joking about killing Trudy a few weeks ago. But seriously, if you get me her address I'll not only kill her, I'll get your money back."

"Not necessary. And anyway, the WitSec deal was a one and done."

"We should call her."

I hold my hand out, and she returns the burner phone. I stare at it and frown. "I don't have her number on this phone. I'll have to get it from my personal phone. Be right back."

"I got this," Callie says, and startles me by reciting Dani's number.

"How do you know her number by heart?"

She shrugs. "I'm gifted."

When Dani answers I say, "What's up?"

"Hi Donovan," she says, sadly. "I'm rage-eating a tub of ice cream, watching TV. I can't believe those bastards kidnapped Analise. I'm devastated."

"Do you *know* her?"

"Are you *kidding*? *Everyone* knows her. She's a national treasure! I *idolize* her. I'm totally obsessed."

"What does that mean?"

"It means I know everything about her. Every detail of her life. I've read her book, and every article she's ever written and every article that's ever been written about her. I follow her on social media. I buy her products. Well, at least the ones I can afford."

"I get it. You like her. I do, too. So anyway, here's the reason I'm calling: it's time."

"Excuse me?"

"It's time, Dani."

"Time for what?" she asks. Then says, "Oh, shit. You don't mean...you're not talking about the..."

"Ultimate Favor? As a matter of fact, I am."

The clattering sound tells me she dropped her phone. When she gets back on she says, "As I recall, you gave me a pass on the favor thingy."

"I did. But as *I* recall, you called me back and said your conscience was bothering you, and that you didn't feel right denying me the favor, since we had a deal."

"Yes, but—"

"You only asked that the favor wouldn't involve forcing you to kill someone. You'll be pleased to hear that while this particular favor doesn't require murder, it's quite important to us."

"Us?"

Callie chimes in. "Hi Dani. It's me, Callie Carpenter. What Donovan's saying, we're in a jam. We need your help."

For a long moment, Dani says nothing. But eventually she whispers: "Please don't tell me you're the ones...who...kidnapped..." Her words die off in the air. Then she whispers, "Analise Compton."

I laugh. "Are you *crazy*? Jesus, Dani! How can you possibly think that?"

"Um..."

"What's wrong?"

"I notice you didn't say no."

"Then please allow me to set the record straight. The answer's no. We didn't kidnap Analise Compton."

She lets out a deep breath. "Thank God! What do you need me to do?"

"Do you own any secluded property?"

"No."

"Think harder."

"I don't own any property of any kind."

"Who do you know that does?"

When she fails to respond, Callie says, "What about Sophie?"

Dani says, "Sofe has a cabin outside Gatlinburg, but it's not what I'd call secluded. It's in a neighborhood"

I ask, "Is anyone using it?"

"Currently? No."

"I'll need the address and a key, and you'll need to meet me there. And when I leave you're going to remain for a certain period of time."

"I am?"

"Yes."

"How long?"

"I don't know. Possibly several weeks."

"Donovan, I can't just—" Her voice drops off. "Okay. I'll work it out."

"Yes, you will. But you can't tell Sophie."

"That's impossible! It's her place. She's got the only key."

"Then you'll need to steal it, make a copy, and replace it without letting her find out."

"Even if I manage all that, Sofe and I *live* together. She's not going to let me just leave for several weeks without an explanation."

"I agree. You'll have to break up with her."

"What? That's crazy!"

"You can get back together after the fact."

"That's unacceptable."

"*Really*, Dani? Because if it's truly unacceptable I can swing by your house and slit Sophie's throat. Would that be easier for you?"

"No."

"Then do your fucking job, Dani. I can't tell you how lucky you are to get such an easy favor. It's the first one I've ever collected that doesn't involve killing someone."

"Thank you for that," she says. "You're right. I'm sorry." After a moment of silence, she adds "Can I ask you something?"

"Go ahead."

"What's the part you *haven't* told me?"

"You'll know soon enough."

She sighs. "When is all this going to take place?"

"You'll steal the key today and meet me at the cabin tomorrow night."

"Okay."

"Dani?"

"Yes?"

"Don't fuck this up."

"I won't."

I end the call and start making breakfast for the three of us. Callie busies herself with destroying the phone, then gets Analise to make a list of the products she wants. When the food's ready, Callie makes a plate for Analise and takes it to her. Before she gets back to the kitchen I get a call on my personal phone.

It's Rose Stout.

When I answer, she says, "We've got a slight problem."

"How slight?"

"It didn't go well."

"What didn't?"

"Hawley's performance."

"She did the talent show?"

"She did."

"What happened?"

"They cut her segment immediately after taping it. But a production assistant made a copy and posted it on YouTube."

"I'll ask you again: what happened?"

Rose says, "I'll text you the link. Watch it, then call me back."

By the time I pull up the link, Callie's back in the kitchen, ready to eat. "What are you watching?"

"I'm not sure yet. Hawley went on that show, *America Loves Talent*. Her segment got cut, but someone posted it on YouTube. Want to watch it with me?"

"How could I possibly say no after such a buildup?"

I press the arrow, and...

Chapter 9

THE SHOW, *AMERICA Loves Talent*, is set in a large theater. There's a stage, an audience, an MC, and three judges: two women and a man. The women are eye candy and the man, Geoffrey, is a pompous narcissist who's famously rude to people whose acts he considers subpar. As the video rolls, and Hawley walks across the stage to the microphone, Callie says, "Omigod! She's *adorable*!"

The audience agrees. They're cheering like crazy.

"They love her already," Callie says.

"They certainly *seem* to. But *why*? She hasn't done anything yet."

"They see a tiny, confident, 6-year-old. It's endearing. They want her to do well."

Maybe so, but Geoffrey doesn't share their opinion. "All right, all right, calm down," he growls to the audience, clearly annoyed by the attention Hawley's getting.

Mindy, one of the judges, admonishes him and calls him a Grinch.

He frowns at her, then turns his attention to Hawley and gives her a stern look. "What's your name, Young Lady?"

"Hawley Stout."

"And how old are you?"

"Six."

When the audience claps, Geoffrey rolls his eyes. "Let's get on with it. I understand you're a magician?"

"No, Sir."

He looks at an index card. "You're not?"

"No."

"I suppose that explains why you don't have any props. If you're not a magician, what are you?"

"A person that does magic."

Perturbed, Geoffrey takes a deep breath. "Isn't that what magicians do?"

"No, Sir."

"What's the difference?"

"Magicians do tricks. I do magic."

The audience goes wild, and Callie explains why: "She's so brave. Totally unafraid of Geoffrey."

Callie's right. Then again, I suppose it's easy to be brave when you can give people an angry look and make their heads explode.

Geoffrey says, "I should probably point out that I don't believe in magic."

"That's okay," Hawley says. "You will by the time I'm finished."

"I sincerely doubt that. Go ahead then, do something magic."

"What would you like me to do?"

"Are you actually going to stand there and tell me you didn't bother to prepare an act? How did you get past our screeners?"

"I told them what they had for breakfast."

"That's not magic," Geoffrey sniffs.

Mindy says, "*I* think it is! Can you tell me what *I* had for breakfast this morning?"

"An egg-white omelet and a piece of toast," Hawley says. "But that's not magic, because it's the same thing you have every day. Magic is making you have something different tomorrow."

Mindy laughs, "And what would *that* be?"

"Four bowls of oatmeal."

Mindy frowns. "Well, I'm afraid you're not very good at this, because I detest oatmeal."

"Not tomorrow," Hawley says.

The audience laughs.

Hawley says, "Tomorrow morning you're gonna love oatmeal. You'll be so hungry for oatmeal nothing else will do. You'll see."

Geoffrey says, "Are you trying to *hypnotize* her?"

"No, Sir. Hypnosis isn't magic. Magic is making her like oatmeal."

Geoffrey glares at the camera. "This is a colossal waste of time. "I'm sorry, Hawley, but when you come on *this* stage, you have to have an *act*. You have to be *prepared*. Since you *weren't*, I'm giving you an X." He leans forward and presses a buzzer, and a portion of the audience says, "Awww."

Geoffrey shrugs.

Hawley says, "That's okay. You'll change your mind. And when you do..." She holds her hand by her ear and spreads her thumb and pinky finger so it looks like she's holding a phone... "Call me!"

The audience erupts with applause.

Geoffrey says, "Go away, Little Girl. We're done here."

But the third judge, Jamie, says, "Can you do something magic right now?"

"Yes, Ma'am. What would you like me to do?"

"I have a secret wish. Do you know what it is?"

"You have lots of wishes. Want me to tell the most important one?"

"If you can."

"You wish you had a baby girl."

Jamie does a double-take. Mindy says, "Is that true?"

Jamie nods. "Well," she says, "that's a lovely thought, but my doctor says I can't have children."

Hawley points at her and says, "You'll have your little girl in September. On a Sunday."

After the audience claps with polite applause, Geoffrey sneers, "This is utter nonsense. Tell us something no one could possibly know."

"I know where Analise Compton is."

The audience gasps.

"Las Vegas," she says.

Geoffrey glares at her. "That's not funny in the least. And it's certainly not magic to make wild claims that can't be proven. And furthermore, it's cruel. If you really want us to believe you can perform magic, give us world peace."

Hawley says, "I can only do things to people I can see."

"Very well. Can you see *me*?"

"Yes, Sir."

"Can you make me fly?"

Hawley cocks her head. "Would you *like* to fly?"

Geoffrey rolls his eyes. "Sure, why not?"

Hawley nods, and Geoffrey yelps in surprise as he instantly rises 20 feet above his chair. As he screams, she holds up her finger and uses it to guide him in a wide circle before depositing him on the judge's table.

"Omigod!" Mindy says, pointing at his crotch.

Geoffrey looks down. He's pissed himself.

As the audience responds with a mixture of concern and approval, Mindy and Jamie stare at him bug-eyed. Geoffrey yells for security to remove her from the stage, and yells, "You'll never be on this show as long as you live!"

Hawley says, "I'm already on the show. Enjoy your oatmeal, Mindy."

As she's being escorted off the stage by security, Geoffrey demands that the cameramen destroy all the footage they shot.

Callie and I look at each other, stunned.

She says, "How'd she know about Analise?"

"Same way she knows where Trudy is."

"Maybe you better call Rose."

I do, on speaker, and she says, "Hawley's tuned into you, Donovan. She knows everything you're doing, in real time."

"How's that possible?"

"She's a witch."

Callie says, "If she knows about Analise, she's a loose end."

Rose says, "Don't even think about it."

I say, "How did this happen, Rose? I thought you had this talent show thing in check."

"I did. She was supposed to make Geoffrey disappear."

"Well, she didn't. She made him fly and piss his pants, and–wait: what do you mean 'make him disappear?'"

"Well, 'disappear' isn't completely accurate. But that's how it would have appeared to the audience."

"So, it's a trick."

"We don't do tricks, Donovan. Geoffrey wouldn't have *gone* anywhere, it's just that no one could have *seen* him."

"Why not?"

"She was going to make him invisible."

"Invisible from their angle of site?"

"From every angle."

"Invisible for *real*? Clothes and everything?"

"Yes, of course."

I take a moment to process. "Rose, that's crazy."

"We're witches, Donovan. You *know* that."

"I've always known you were incredibly gifted, but–"

"This can't possibly come as a shock to you. It's the reason you let me adopt Hawley."

"Look: I know you've always *called* yourselves witches. But it was a figure of speech."

"Figure of *speech*? *You* call us witches!"

"Yes, but it's like a term of endearment, like the octogenarian women who meet for lunch and call each other bitches. They don't expect people to believe they're literally the offspring of *dogs*! Sure, we say you and Hawley are witches, but–"

"If we're not witches, what are we?"

"Incredibly gifted."

"You mean like people who excel at math or piano? Hawley can blow people's *heads* off their shoulders!"

I notice Callie's jaw has dropped. She whispers, "What the *fuck*?"

Rose says, "Look, you want to call us gifted, that's fine with me. It's certainly safer."

"In what way?"

"No one burns chess champions at the stake."

"Good point. Why would Hawley rat me out about Analise Compton?"

"She didn't. She only said that Analise was in Las Vegas."

"Is that all she knows?"

"I have no clue what she knows."

"Why not? You're both witches, aren't you?"

"You and Callie are both humans. Does that mean you know everything she knows?"

"Let's start over," I say. "You're telling me that you and Hawley are certified, honest-to-God witches, and that witches–like the kind from the 1600's–are real."

"That's correct. Except that no one certifies witches. By the way, humans aren't certified either, far as I know."

"Can she really make people invisible?"

"Yes."

"Can *you* do it?"

"Who do you think taught Hawley?"

Callie says, "This is bullshit, Donovan. She's fucking with you."

"I don't think so. *Are* you?"

"No," Rose says. "And Callie knows better than to doubt my word. Ask her about the time she saw me in Manhattan, and tried to follow me: I froze her in her tracks."

"Let's concentrate on this invisible thing."

"It's pretty basic. What you might call Witchcraft 101."

"Where are you now?"

"Los Angeles. That's where they taped the show."

"I need you in Las Vegas."

"When?"

"Right now."

"Hawley can't teleport. She'll have to fly."

"She can *fly*?"

"On a *plane*, Donovan."

"Oh. Right."

"What did you picture, a broomstick?"

"Well, you said you were witches."

"Witches, not stereotypes."

Chapter 10

"*WARWICK & POST*," Callie says, exiting Analise's bedroom.

"Excuse me?"

She holds up a sheet of paper. "The products Analise requested."

"The ones from Europe?"

"Uh huh."

"Do they sell them in Las Vegas?"

"Are you kidding? You can buy *anything* in Las Vegas!"

She grabs a bottle of water from the fridge, sits on one of the barstools at the kitchen counter, and taps on her phone. After a minute she says, "Here we go: they sell *Warwick & Post* at the Fashion Show Mall."

"If you want to go shopping, I can stay here and guard her."

"How long before Rose and Hawley get here?"

"Three hours."

"I might do that. I'd like Analise to have her products before you leave, since you're not gonna find them in Gatlinburg."

"Are you planning to buy some for yourself?"

"I might. I like what she said about them."

Callie and I have the ability to sit quietly for long periods of time without feeling the need to maintain a conversation. We'd be doing that right now, under normal circumstances. But hearing Rose say my daughter can make people invisible, Callie wants to know if I believe her.

"Not for a second," I say. "Do you?"

"No. It's impossible."

We're quiet again till Callie says, "So why did you send for them? You're delaying your trip by hours."

I shrug. "I miss Hawley. I haven't seen her in months."

"So, just to clarify: your plan *doesn't* rely on Hawley making Analise invisible."

I laugh. "Actually, that *is* the plan: we'll visit for a while, and when it's time to go, Hawley will make her invisible, I'll charter a private jet, Analise will walk out the door with us, you'll drive us to the airport, and she and I will walk right into the private jet. We'll fly to Nashville, I'll rent a car and drive her the rest of the way."

"And if she *can't* make Analise invisible?"

"I'll rent a van, stuff her back in the trunk, and you and I will hoist the trunk into the back of the van."

"While hoping no one sees us loading a huge, heavy trunk into the back of the van in broad daylight."

"Exactly."

"And then?"

"I'll drive her to Gatlinburg."

"Question?"

"Please."

"Assuming the impossible occurs, and Hawley can make her invisible, what makes you think Analise will go quietly to the airport and climb into the jet?"

"Two things: one, I'll convince her if she makes a sound, I'll kill her. And two, she hates being drugged, and would love to avoid being stuck in a trunk for 30 hours."

"Is that how long it takes to drive to Gatlinburg?"

I nod.

"If she's invisible, how can you keep her from running away first chance she gets?"

"We'll keep the bracelet on her and program it to my phone. If she strays more than 20 feet from me, she'll blow her leg off."

"You trust Dani to steal Sophie's key and break up with her?"

"I trust her to try."

Callie takes a deep breath before saying, "I know Sophie's related to Sal Bonadello."

"She's his only niece, and he adores her."

"Right. And Sal gives us mob jobs from time to time."

"Where are you going with this?"

"I could fly to Nashville and kill Sophie. That would solve Dani's problems. Sal would never suspect *us*, because we're always there for him. In fact, he'll probably hire *you* to find Sophie's killer."

"We don't need to kill Sophie."

"What makes you so certain?"

"I've got a plan for that."

Callie frowns. "Another plan?"

"You don't trust me?"

"I do. But it's not just your ass on the line here. We could do life for this."

"Don't be silly. We'll be dead long before this case ever gets to trial."

Callie thinks a moment. "Since we don't believe she'll be made invisible, maybe you should go ahead and rent a van, just in case."

"You're probably right. Will you be okay here for a while?"

"Of course."

"Anything you need while I'm out?"

"Nope. I'm good."

Chapter 11

AFTER RENTING A van and parking it in one of the many empty parking spaces in Callie's garage, I ring her bell and she presses a button to unlock the elevator access. After letting me in her penthouse I ask what's happened in the news. She says the president made a public statement.

"What was his demeanor?"

"Anger, fear, concern. All the emotions you'd expect from a normal, loving father."

"I suppose she's the one thing he truly cares about. Is Analise's plan working?"

"Like you wouldn't believe!"

"Tell me."

"The whole government seems to have shut down. The whole world, even. The outpouring of support is off the charts. It's like the guy suddenly woke up with no enemies. Both parties are in a state of shock. She's really quite beloved."

"You think he's in on it?"

"The president? No way."

"He couldn't be acting?"

"*This* guy?" She laughs. "He's the world's worst actor. He was choking back tears. In his mind, this is definitely real."

We walk into the kitchen, and she turns up the volume on the TV. When a commercial comes on she asks, "If you could have any super power, what would it be?"

I ask, "How long have you been thinking about this?"

"The whole time you were gone."

"What did you come up with?"

"Invincibility: the power to not be physically harmed. What about you?"

"I like this thing we're hoping to see from Hawley: the ability to make myself and others invisible."

"Why?"

"It's perfect for our business. If I could've made myself invisible yesterday I could've followed Analise into the bathroom and given her an injection to make her unconscious. Then I could've made *her* invisible and carried her out the door on my shoulder."

"The Secret Service guy would've seen the door open when you left."

"Not if I waited for *you* to enter the bathroom before carrying her out."

She frowns. "If you could make yourself invisible you wouldn't need your mini surveillance cameras. You could voyeur women day and night."

"That's a harsh comment to make."

"Don't try denying it. The list of names is too long."

"I agree it's a long list. But I'm sure you know it includes more men than women. And there was a valid business reason for each one."

"What about the bathroom cams?"

I shrug. "It's an intrusive business."

"Uh huh."

Callie goes shopping and gets back before Rose and Hawley arrive. With nothing else to do, I follow Callie into the bedroom to see how Analise reacts.

She's elated.

Over soap products and personal items.

Go figure.

Ten minutes later Rose calls to say she and Hawley can't come to Vegas.

Shit. "Why not?"

"We've been asked to remain at the hotel."

"By whom?"

"The police."

"Why?"

"Apparently, they saw the video where Hawley said Analise was in Vegas."

"She's a child on a talent show! Why would they take her seriously?"

"Because they talked to Geoffrey, and he confirmed she made him levitate. Now, the FBI wants to interview us."

"Fuck!"

"Tell me about it."

"Can you control Hawley during the interview?"

"I think so. Provided they don't say anything to piss her off."

Chapter 12

I WALK BACK into the bedroom and give Analise the bad news. "I'm afraid you'll have to get back in the trunk."

Her gigantic eyes grow even larger. "*Why?*"

"We have to move you."

"Why?"

"The FBI has reason to believe you're in Las Vegas."

"*Please* don't drug me again! I swear I'll cooperate!"

"I believe you. After all, your father can't benefit politically if you're rescued too quickly. So, I'll make you a deal: I won't drug you, provided you get in the trunk and remain quiet until I let you out."

"When will that be?"

"As soon as we get out of the city."

"After that, we're done with the trunk forever, okay?"

"I'm afraid I can't make *that* promise, since I have to get you out of the van and into your next location undetected. But if you cooperate fully, that should be the only time, and it shouldn't take more than a couple of minutes."

"You promise?"

"I do."

"Can I ride in the passenger seat?"

"No."

She thinks about it, then says, "Should I worry?"

"About what?"

"Why you're being so accommodating?"

"I'm being practical: we've got a 30-hour drive ahead of us, and you'll need to relieve yourself several times along the way. If I drug you, I'll have to pull over every hour to make sure you haven't pissed or shit yourself, and when you finally do, I'll have to clean you up and deal with the smell. The trunk is *supposed* to be waterproof, but who knows? If it's not, your excrement will leak into the rental van and I'll have to scrub and disinfect the carpet for hours before turning it back in. But all this unpleasantness can be avoided by not drugging you in the first place. If you're conscious, I can pull over whenever you need to relieve yourself."

"Where are we going?"

"Gatlinburg, Tennessee."

"Wow! *That's* a surprise."

"You like Gatlinburg?"

"I don't know, I've never been there. I'm just surprised you'd tell me where you're taking me."

I shrug. "I'm just saving you the trouble of worrying about it. You'd eventually figure it out anyway."

"What do you mean?"

"You'll be able to see the signs all the way there. You won't be in the passenger seat, but you'll still be able to see out the front windshield."

Callie says, "Can we talk?"

I follow her to the kitchen, where she says, "This is all for her benefit, right?"

"What do you mean?"

"Tell me you're not seriously planning to drive her all the way to Tennessee."

"What else would I do?"

"Drive her to the desert, kill her, and move on with your life."

"Normally I would. But I want to see how this plays out."

Callie clenches her teeth. "There are way too many people involved in this deal. On her end–at the very least–you've got her husband, Randy; and the general; and the lady you called on the phone that you found in the boot; and the ones who'll be posing as the kidnappers making demands from various parts of the country. And on our end–even though we killed Alma, her boyfriend, two detectives, and the neighborhood association guy–we still have three others with direct knowledge of the kidnapping: Anson, Hawley, and Rose. And soon that list will include Dani Ripper. You say you've got a plan for Sophie? Fine. But if you're wrong, she's another loose end."

"What are you suggesting?"

"I think we need to cut and run."

"Why?"

"Because this whole deal has been hinky from the start."

"I agree. But I don't want to kill her till I know why the general wants her dead."

"But you agree she needs to die eventually, correct? Otherwise, we'll never be safe."

"Of course."

"Promise me you'll kill her."

"I promise."

"Thank you. Now tell me what I can do to help."

"She'll need provisions for the trip: bottled water, snacks, a sleeping bag, clean clothes, personal products..."

"I'll put all that together and toss in a week's worth of clothes. If she's still alive by the time she runs out of clean clothes, Dani can wash them at Sophie's place." She laughs.

"What's so funny?"

"I'm sure Sophie's cabin has a washer and dryer, but I just had this vision of Dani Ripper wading in the waters of Dudley Creek, washing my clothes and beating them with a rock."

While Callie packs everything Analise might need, I flip the channels on her kitchen TV to find the media coverage relentless. Every channel has a panel of so-called "experts" who are dissecting and parsing every possible angle of the kidnapping and explaining what it might mean for the presidency. I settle on a channel showing a freeze-frame of Hawley, and turn the sound up in time to hear the host say there's a rumor the FBI may have located someone with direct knowledge of the kidnapping. He wonders aloud if the rumor has anything to do with the video that surfaced earlier today. Then he shows Hawley's audition tape.

PART 6

Creed & Analise

Chapter 1

THE DRIVE IS mind-numbing. Thankfully, Analise is smart enough to know I'm bored, angry, and totally uninterested in conversation. She asks for only two things: the occasional bathroom break, and an hourly five-minute news update on the radio. In the meantime, she's content to remain quiet in the back of the van and listen to the old-fogey music stations I discover along the way. Every few hours I ask if she's okay, and she says, "Yes, thank you." On one occasion she adds, "I just miss my family."

She's an easy travel companion. I like that about her...

And I genuinely like *her*.

Chapter 2

IT TAKES US sixteen hours to get to Oklahoma City, where I stop to fill the gas tank for the third time. As always, Analise hides under the blanket. After pumping the gas, I walk next door and pick up some food and laugh at the expression on Analise's face when I hand her a burger, fries, and a chocolate shake.

"You're joking," she says, but scarfs them down before I get back on the Interstate.

"Was that your first Whopper?"

"What do you mean?"

"That's the burger you just ate. It's called a Whopper. How'd you like it?"

"It was surprisingly good. Or maybe I was just starving." She pauses. "You know what else surprises me? You haven't asked a single thing about my father."

"Why would I?"

"Because *everyone* does. Surely there must be *one* thing you'd like to know about him."

I think about it a moment. "If I ask you something, will you promise to answer truthfully?"

"Yes."

"Here's what I want to know: in his lifetime, has your father ever been inside a grocery store?"

She howls with laughter. "*That's* what you want to know?"

"That's it."

"You're crazy!"

"What's the answer?"

"To the best of my knowledge, no. He's never stepped foot inside a grocery store."

"Even as a child?"

"Especially as a child."

We ride an hour or so in silence. Then, abruptly, she says, "Can I ask *you* a question?"

"Go for it."

"You're quite good-looking."

"That's your question?"

"No. My question is, why do you consort with prostitutes?"

I smile. "Consort?"

"It means to habitually associate with–"

"I know what it means, Analise. My answer is, with a hooker, you always know where you stand. There are emotional games, of course, but you know going in that it's just her, trying to make you feel special. You both know why you're there, and you have no false illusions about the relationship. She won't ask embarrassing or personal questions, and doesn't care what you do before you show up or after you leave. There's no pressure to perform because you know going in she's going to fake her orgasm. And there's this: I don't have to worry she might cheat on me when I leave, or that she'll say or do something that could get her killed. When it comes to sex, I can tell her what I like without worrying if she'll think less of me."

"It sounds dreadful."

"I'm sure it does. But I'm not ashamed to admit that some of the best times of my life took place in the company of hookers. And I'm not just talking about sex. A good hooker can change a man's life."

"How?"

"By listening to his problems without judging him, and by comforting him during his worst times. A good hooker will always make him feel special. Like he *means* something to her, even if it's a short period of time."

"But it's not *real*."

"How many marriages are real?"

"I honestly don't know. But *mine* is."

"That's a wonderful thing to say. I hope you're right."

"You sound skeptical."

"Of *your* marriage? Not at all. I only know *my* marriage fell short of our original hopes and dreams."

"Maybe you should have treated her better. Why are you laughing?"

"I think you might want to work on your kidnap banter."

"What do you mean?"

"It's generally unwise to criticize a guy who's been paid to kill you. But you're right. I'm sure I could've treated her better. Still, it's interesting you assumed our divorce was *my* fault."

"I'm sorry. I'm sure that came across as gender-based, but I was really thinking about your profession. You have a very stressful job."

"You mean because I kill people for a living I'm probably the type of guy that abused his wife?"

"No, of *course* not! I didn't mean to imply..." She pauses. "You're right. I need to work on my kidnap banter."

We drive in silence until I say, "I'm sure I'm not easy to live with."

She says nothing, and remains quiet for nearly two hours. Then she says, "Does this ankle bracelet really contain a bomb?"

"Not a *bomb*, per se. More like a blasting cap. Why do you ask?"

"I was wondering if you could increase my range for the next bathroom break."

"Why?"

"I don't want to be next to the van this time."

"Why not? I can't *see* you."

"I need more privacy." When I fail to respond, she says, "I need to go Number Two."

"I still don't see the problem. First of all, I would never spy on you. Second, I'll be inside, and you'll be outside, on the opposite side of the van, squatting, so I won't even be able to see the top of your head."

"I'm talking about afterward. Every time I pee you wait till I get back in the van, then you drive a few feet, then you stop and get out of the van to look at it."

"What's the problem?"

She frowns. "Why do you like to stare at my pee?"

I laugh. "I'm not staring at your pee. I'm making sure you didn't leave a message."

"What do you mean?"

"When you pee, you're outside the van, by the road. You could grab a stick or rock and write a message underneath the van and I'd never know."

"You can't be serious!"

"Help! I'm Analise Compton. I've been kidnapped by Donovan Creed. He's taking me to Gatlinburg, Tennessee."

"That's an awfully long message."

"Maybe so, but I doubt anyone could accuse you of being a fast pisser. If I were a better kidnapper I'd stand in front of you and watch you like a hawk."

Her eyes grow large. "That would be a *terrible* invasion of my privacy."

"I agree. Which is why I haven't."

"And I appreciate that. But still, I'd prefer you don't look at my poop."

"Do you really think I care what your poop looks like?"

"I honestly don't know. But I don't want you looking at it. What if I promise not to leave a message?"

"Not good enough."

"This is important to me, Mr. Creed."

"I can see that. Look: you originally asked if I can give you a wider area. I can."

"How wide an area?"

"It's tricky setting the range outdoors, but I'm sure I can give you a circle of at least 150 feet."

"Thank you. And just this once, will you trust me not to leave a message if I promise not to?"

"I'll consider it."

"Thank you."

Chapter 3

AT THE FIRST opportunity, I turn off the Interstate and follow the main road till I get to a farm road, which I follow until I'm certain there's no one within miles. Then I make a u-turn, pull over, exit the van, walk a hundred feet or so, and use my phone to set the range. Noticing the area is entirely covered in grass and thickets, I can see there's not much danger of her scratching out a message.

Now, back in the van, I say, "I've given you a wide range. Try to stay within 150 feet of the van. There's plenty of brush to hide behind, but be quick."

She grabs a roll of toilet paper, gets out, does her business, comes back, gets back in the van, and looks me in the eyes.

I know what she wants.

She wants me to trust her. To drive away without checking to see if she left a message beside her poop. I stare back into her eyes and see no trace of guile. When I shift my gaze to her mouth her famous lips part the slightest bit, leaving me with the overwhelming feeling we've reached a critical moment in our relationship.

She's testing me.

If I drive away she'll know I trust her. If I leave the van to check for messages, she'll know I *don't* trust her, which means she can't trust *me*. I look out my window a moment. Then, against my better judgement, I start the car and drive to the main road, turn right, and head to the Interstate.

"Thanks, Donovan," she says.

Donovan.

Not Mr. Creed this time.

Donovan.

My reward for trusting her.

Just as I'm about to merge onto the Interstate, I turn the car around.

"What's wrong?" she asks.

Without responding, I drive all the way back to the place we stopped. Ignoring her sigh of disappointment, I get out, walk to the last place I saw her standing before she squatted behind some shrubbery. I search a thirty-foot radius until I finally see a pile of poop. But it's horse poop, not human, and it's old, and located beside what appears to be a horse trail. Also visible is a pair of pale blue panties with a message written in lipstick: *Donovan Creed kidnapped Analise Compton. DNA.* There's a circle after the word DNA, and a wet spot where I assume she spit.

I stuff the panties in my pocket and walk back to the van and say nothing till we stop for gas in Little Rock. "Do you need anything?" I ask.

"No, thank you."

After filling the tank, I get back in the van and say, "I thought the kidnapping was your idea."

"It was."

"If that's true, it's to your advantage not to be rescued until you're ready."

"I agree."

"Then why would you leave a pair of panties with your DNA telling people I kidnapped you?"

"I had several reasons."

"Name one."

"I wanted to know if I could trust you not to check up on me."

"As it turned out, you weren't worthy of that trust. Give me another reason."

"You were ordered to kill me. So far, you haven't. But if you decide to, I'd prefer you don't get away with it."

"I notice you didn't say we were heading to Gatlinburg. Why?"

"Like you said, I don't want to be rescued until it's time."

"Here's my problem, Analise: if I *don't* kill you, and your plan works to perfection, these panties would've been out there, linking me to your kidnapping."

"But you found them, so it's a moot point."

"You took a big chance. Why'd you do it?"

"The panties were going to be my insurance policy."

"What do you mean?"

"If the plan worked, and you didn't kill me, I would've told you about the panties. But if you *did* kill me, I figured someone would eventually find them, and they'd come looking for you."

"What if someone happened to find them right away?"

"Highly unlikely in such a remote area. But it was a risk I was willing to take."

I continue driving until Analise tells me she needs to go Number Two.

"*This* again?"

"For real," she says.

This time after pulling over, I open my door and say, "Okay, let's go."

"What are you doing?" she says.

"Escorting you."

"Why?"

"*You* know why."

"You're not planning to–"

"I am indeed, so deal with it."

"Unacceptable."

Seeing she has no intention of leaving the van, I say, "My uncle was a vibrant man before his accident."

"What?"

"He got run over by his own tractor. Wound up a quadriplegic."

"And you're telling me this because?"

"I lived with him for several months after the accident. It's a myth that attendants extract the stools manually."

"I'm sorry. *What?*"

"Each day I sat him on an elevated toilet seat that was high enough to make his ass accessible from below. Then I had to insert my finger deep into his rectum and swirl it around to stimulate the bowels and relax his sphincter. Then the stool fell out naturally. But that's not the only way to do it. There's a bearing down technique called the Valsalva maneuver, but that requires cooperation. Before we got the elevated seat I had to turn him on his side, bend his knees, and physically dig the stools from his rectum."

"Omigod! What are you trying to *say?*"

"I can either *watch* you shit, or *make* you shit. Your choice."

Now, standing in front of her as she defecates, I can see she's mortified.

"Enjoying the view?" she asks, with great sarcasm.

"Don't flatter yourself."

"You're a pig of a man," she says. As the tears stream down her face she says, "This is sexual harassment."

I sigh. "That's a stretch. You've got a blanket wrapped around you. It's not like I can *see* anything."

"You can't *possibly* understand how degrading this is."

"Would it help if I shit in front of *you*?" I start to unbuckle my belt.

"Don't you *dare*!" she shouts. "Omigod! I can't believe we're even *having* this conversation. In my whole life I've never met anyone so foul. I can't believe people like you even *exist* in the world."

My phone vibrates.

It's Callie.

Before answering, I tell Analise: "I get that you've led a sheltered, privileged life, and never had to shit outdoors with people around. I suggest you consider this a learning experience. I'll bet the kids who work in your overseas sweatshops don't get this much privacy when *they* shit."

"Fuck *you*!

"Thanks for the offer, but as pretty as you are, this isn't the proper setting. When we get to Gatlinburg, after you get cleaned up, I'll consider it." I toss her the toilet paper, but she fumbles the catch and bats it about six feet away. I laugh, and click on the phone to answer the call as Analise lunges toward the toilet paper, seemingly oblivious that the blanket has fallen away from her body to expose most of her bare ass. Surprisingly, she doesn't cover herself. "Give me just a sec," I tell Callie.

My natural inclination is—as Analise suggested earlier—to enjoy the view. But this is so out of Analise's character, I overlook her vertical smile and focus on her hands. Thankfully, I'm able—just barely—to dodge the sizeable rock she hurled at my face.

Now she covers up, so I ask Callie, "What's up?"

"Kidnapping," she says.

"What about it?"

"We *suck* at it. Never again, okay?"

"Okay. What happened?"

"Karen and Cubby just tried to kill me."

"Who?"

Chapter 4

"TWO HITMEN," CALLIE says. "They call themselves Karen and Cubby, from some old Disney TV show."

"Let me get this straight: two hitmen just showed up out of the blue? At your place?"

"They were posing as husband and wife. Said they were negotiating to buy one of the condos in the building and wanted to ask me some questions."

"They had no idea you own all the condos?"

"Nope."

"How'd you disable them?"

"The new spray you gave me."

"Did they vomit?"

"The guy did. She did too, but that was later, during the interrogation."

"Where are they now?"

"Hanging upside down, naked, from a beam in my theater room."

"You got them to talk?"

She laughs. "What do *you* think?"

"What'd you learn?"

"They came to kill Analise."

As I take a moment to think about what she just said, Callie adds, "You're wondering how they knew she was alive, and why they thought she was at my place, right?"

"Not really. I assume someone told the general about Hawley's video. He doesn't know she's my kid, and doesn't know if Analise is alive, but he *does* know you and I kidnapped her, and that you live in Vegas. So, when a kid made the national news saying Analise was alive, in Vegas, he sent two killers to check it out."

Callie says, "Not even close."

I hear a sudden scream in the background. Callie says, "I'll be right back." While I wait for her to return I keep a close watch on Analise, to make sure the only thing that comes out from under her blanket in her hand is toilet paper. When Callie gets back on the phone I ask, "Who hired Karen and Cubby?"

"Our old friend, Carmine Porrello. But he never told them who I was."

I laugh. "Of course, he didn't! You're a legend in the business. If they knew it was you they would've shit their pants and never showed up!" I pause. "I'm going to put you on speaker so Analise can hear what you've learned. Give me just a sec." I move closer to Analise, put the phone on speaker and say, "Okay, go ahead."

Callie says, "Analise, two professional killers showed up at my place a half hour ago. They were hired by a local mob boss who told them to kill you on sight."

"I don't believe you," Analise says.

I ask, "How did they track Analise to your place?"

"Remember her *Warwick & Post* products? You can only buy them online, or in a handful of American stores. Someone—I assume the general—told Analise to ask for them by name after getting kidnapped. He apparently had someone monitoring the sales, and when I bought the items with my credit card, they knew Analise was alive. They called Carmine, and he hired the killers."

"So, Analise thought the soap products would allow the general to help her, but in reality he used them to make sure she was *dead*?"

"Exactly."

Again, Analise says, "I don't believe you!"

Callie says, "Believe whatever you want. But if you're into bondage nudity I'll be glad to text you their photos."

"Please do," I say.

When they show up on my phone, I study them carefully. "Are they local?"

"Yeah. They work out of Henderson."

"What are their real names?"

She tells me. I ask, "Ever heard of them?"

"Nope. You?"

"No. How skilled are they?"

"Compared to *us*?" Callie says. "Bush league."

"You know what bothers me?"

"I do," she says. "The general and his people have been one step ahead of us the whole time. Which is why we suck at kidnapping."

PART 7

Creed, Analise, & Dani Ripper

Chapter 1

NINE HOURS LATER we pull in front of Sophie Alexander's cabin in Gatlinburg, Tennessee. Dani was right: it's not super secluded, but it *is* nighttime, and these are vacation cabins, and they're out of season, which makes this an excellent place to keep Analise.

After locking her in the trunk, I call Dani and have her open the garage door. Since there's only one bay, she has to move her car to make room for the van. After she does, I back the van into the garage. After parking her car in the driveway, Dani comes into the garage to help me. Dani being Dani, she thinks the trunk contains a dead body. I explain it's a world-famous multi-millionaire who's alive and well, but wishes not to be seen by the locals. Dani shuts the garage door and helps me lift the trunk out the back and up the four steps that lead to the kitchen hallway. Once inside, Dani asks, "What's his name?"

"Who are we talking about?"

"The guy in the trunk. The multi-millionaire. It's Mark Cuban, right?"

I show her a look of complete surprise. "How'd you guess?"

"It *is* Mark Cuban? Holy *shit*!"

"It's not Mark Cuban." As I unlock the latches I suddenly remember telling her I didn't kidnap Analise Compton. With that in mind, I say, "Don't be pissed." Then I open the trunk and study Dani's reaction. At first, she's stunned into silence, which is rare for Dani. But when Analise climbs out of the trunk and puts her hand out for Dani to shake, Dani says, "That's amazing. Astonishing, really."

"What is?"

"The resemblance."

"What do you mean?"

"Other than the eyes, she looks *exactly* like Analise Compton."

"What do you mean?"

"Analise photographs with either blue or green eyes, but those are contact lenses. Her natural eyes are brown. This girl's eyes are green, but she's not wearing contact lenses. Who *is* she?"

"I'm Analise Compton."

Dani smiles. "I have to commend you on your voice."

"Thank you. I've had it all my life."

"No, you haven't."

Analise looks at me. "This is an odd exchange. Are you certain your friend is mentally stable?"

I say, "Dani fancies herself an expert on all things Analise Compton."

"Well, she's certainly wrong about my natural eye color."

"No, I'm not," Dani says.

To Dani, I say: "Ask her something only Analise would know."

Dani thinks a minute, then says, "What's the name of the puppy you got for your sixth birthday?"

"Fluffy."

"Wrong! It was Sir Paul."

Analise bristles. "I ought to know the name of my own dog."

"I agree. You should. But you don't."

"For your information," Analise says, "You're referring to the replacement puppy. The original dog was a Teacup Maltese. White, with a black nose, named Fluffy. Sadly, Fluffy was born with a congenital heart condition, so my father made the breeder exchange her."

"With Sir Paul?"

"That's right."

"Wrong again," Dani says. "Analise Compton never had a pet until she turned twelve. Her parents refused to have animals in the house."

"Then why did I get one on my twelfth birthday?"

"Because that was the year *you*—I mean *Analise*—got a new stepmom who wanted to form a bond. But it didn't work. She never accepted the stepmom. And by the way, Analise got a cat for her twelfth birthday, not a dog. And the cat's name was Skimbleshanks, not Sir Paul."

Analise turns to me. "Is this some sort of joke?"

"You tell me."

"Very well, it's a joke. But it's not funny. If I'm not Analise Compton, why is half the world searching for me?"

I ask Dani: "How many bedrooms do you have?"

"Three."

"Where do you want her?"

"I'm not sure I want her at all."

"Well, you're stuck with her. She'll need a bedroom and a bathroom."

Chapter 2

DANI LEADS US upstairs and says, "Both these bedrooms have a private bathroom."

"They also have windows."

"Every room in the house has at least one window, including the bathrooms."

"Is there a basement?"

"No."

I frown. "I'll have to board these windows up from the outside."

"You can't!" Dani says. "Sophie will freak!"

"I'll restore everything back to its original condition. Sophie will never know unless you tell her. In the meantime, here's what you need to know about your guest: she's wearing an explosive device on her ankle." I walk to the center of the room and calibrate the app on my phone. "I'm setting a radius of twenty feet from this very spot, which will allow her to move freely about this bedroom and bath. She'll also be able to get about three or four feet into the hall, which I'm not happy about."

"What do you mean 'explosive device?'"

"If she goes outside the radius at any time, the device will blow her leg off."

"I can't babysit a woman who's strapped to a *bomb*," Dani says.

"You don't have a choice."

I access my phone contacts and press Callie's name. When she answers, I say, "We're at Sophie's. Thanks to Dani, I finally know why the general wanted me to kill Analise."

"Tell me."

"It's not her."

"Excuse me?"

"This isn't Analise. She's a body-double."

Callie goes silent a moment. Then says, "That makes sense. I kept wondering why Analise Compton would trust killers to kidnap her, and why she'd voluntarily put herself in such a dangerous situation. Also, General Barry used to run Homeland, so he was in the pipeline, same as us. They probably have two or three Analise Comptons floating around."

"Probably. But I bet this one's the best."

"I agree. What gave her away?"

"Eye color and pet history."

"Good for Dani. So, who *is* this woman? Where's she from? How much does she know?"

"So far, she's sticking with her story. But I haven't started interrogating her yet. Rest assured, I'll know soon enough."

"Be forceful."

"Okay. Speaking of which, how are you getting along with Karen and Cubby?"

"Sadly, they didn't make it."

"Did you glean any additional information?"

"Yeah, but just mob stuff."

"Valuable enough to make Carmine leave you alone from here on out?"

"I think so."

"Good. Watch yourself."

"You too. And call me when you get your answers."

"I will."

Chapter 3

I DON'T ENJOY torturing women unless they deserve it, and Analise certainly doesn't. It's obvious she's a civilian, like Punch and Judy, and has been well-paid to play a roll she believes will help our country. Unfortunately for her, body-doubles are highly expendable, and usually killed the moment they've outlived their usefulness. After telling her this, she remains undaunted. "I'm Analise Compton," she says. "I swear it on my life. Your friend, Dani, is wrong."

"Dani's never wrong," I counter.

"You can't find a picture of me with brown eyes, though I did have them as a child. But they changed color as I grew."

"Your eyes changed from brown to green?"

"That's correct. But she's right about one thing: I sometimes wear contacts to make them blue, for photo shoots. And greener, as well."

"What about the pets?"

"She probably got that stuff from pulp magazines. I was just going along with it because you looked like you believed her."

"You were bluffing about Sir Paul?"

"Yes."

"I don't believe you."

"Kill me, then."

"I'd prefer not to, but I'm certainly willing to, if you give me no choice."

"I'm not afraid of you," she says.

"Yes, you are, just as you should be." Having given her fair warning, I go downstairs and tell Dani to go for a drive."

"What are you going to do?"

"Ask her some questions."

She bites her lip. "Donovan? Please don't hurt her."

"I don't *want* to hurt her, but I need some answers."

Dani sighs. "This is all my fault. I never should have told you she was an imposter. The only reason I did was because I believed you when you said you didn't kidnap Analise Compton."

"And I obviously didn't."

"No, but you *thought* you did, which means you knowingly lied to me. I thought we were friends. I would never lie to you."

"Everyone lies."

"I don't. And if you want to continue being my friend you'll swear on your life right now that you'll never lie to me again."

"Are you serious?"

"I am."

"Okay, then."

"Okay, what?"

"We can't be friends."

"What do you mean?"

"I'd be lying if I made that promise."

She looks at me in disbelief. "Is it that hard for you to be honest?"

"I'm being honest right now. Lying's a major part of my life. Callie's, too."

"You don't lie to each other."

"Of course, we do! We *practice* lying to each other. Our ability to lie has saved countless lives over the years, including yours."

"I don't believe that."

"Dani, before you turn your back on our friendship, search your heart. You've lied to me at least twice that I know of, and do I need to remind you the lies you told Sophie when you cheated on her?" When she fails to respond I add, "You love your partner. What's his name? Dillon? How many times have you lied to him?"

"A million."

"And are you still friends?"

She nods.

"Everyone lies," I say.

"Not Dillon. Not to me."

"He lied to you about dating your secretary."

"Just at first."

I smile.

She says, "Okay, you can still be my friend. But don't hurt her."

"Are we talking about the young lady upstairs?"

"Yes. The one with the bomb on her leg."

"Ankle."

"Whatever."

"If you don't want me to hurt her, you'd better tell her to answer my questions."

"Okay." Dani looks at me. "You mean right now?"

I nod.

"Wait here," she says.

When she goes upstairs, I attach an earbud to my phone and tune it to the frequency that matches the bug I placed in Analise's bedroom.

Dani starts by saying, "I'm really sorry I ratted you out."

Analise says, "You didn't rat me out. You just made a mistake." She goes on to tell Dani the same things she told me: that her eyes changed colors over the years and the information Dani must have read about the pets was inaccurate. Dani doesn't argue with her. Instead, she says, "You need to tell Mr. Creed whatever he wants to know. Because if you don't, he'll hurt you."

Analise laughs. "If that were true, he wouldn't have sent you up here to threaten me. He would've already hurt me."

"You're wrong about that. He'll kill you if you don't answer his questions truthfully."

"Look: I know he's supposed to be this big, scary hitman. But he's not going to murder the president's daughter."

"Maybe not. But he'll absolutely murder you."

"I don't think so."

"Please reconsider."

Analise sighs. "You seem like a nice person, Dani, and I'm flattered you've read everything you could find about me. But if you really don't want me to get hurt you should talk to *him*, not me. Because I'm absolutely Analise Compton. And hurting me won't change that."

Before leaving, Dani says, "I'm really sorry I put you in this position."

"Me, too," Analise says.

After Dani leaves, I remove the small leather bag from my luggage that Callie calls my "man purse." I place the shoulder strap around my neck and shoulder, then grab a roll of paper towels from the kitchen, as well as one of Sophie's kitchen chairs, which I carry up the steps.

Without saying a word, I cable wire Analise to the chair and bind her hands behind her back. Then I wire her ankles to the chair legs, making a conscious effort not to cover her ankle bracelet. After showing her the six vials in my leather case, I remove one, along with a scalpel and a small box of matches.

"Will you answer my questions?" I ask.

"Yes."

"Thank you. What's your name?"

"Analise Compton."

I sigh.

Chapter 4

TEN MINUTES LATER, my phone rings.

When I answer, Dani Ripper says, "Donovan! I've been on my phone, checking the Internet. Analise is right! People's eye color *can* change from brown to green as they age."

"Brown to hazel, maybe."

"No! I'm serious! Brown to green. And it's very possible I got the pet stuff wrong. I mean, I probably *did* read that in one of the tabloids. What I'm saying–"

"Dani?"

"Yes?"

"It's too late."

"What do you mean?"

"You know what I mean."

Chapter 5

TEN MINUTES EARLIER…

"The six vials in my case," I tell Analise, "contain ingredients that offer varying degrees of pain. I'm going to start with the first vial, which is by far the easiest to endure. Nevertheless, it's going to be a bitch if you've never experienced torture. Hopefully, we won't have to go beyond that one."

"I don't believe you," she says. "I'm the president's daughter. I've been promised you won't hurt me."

"You were promised that by the man who wants you dead. But enough of that. You've been blessed with a beautiful face and body, and I'd sooner destroy a priceless painting than disfigure you. But we're at an impasse. I need answers, and you refuse to give them. So, I'm no longer threatening you. I will, however, be respectful, and try to limit the damage to areas only a lover might see."

I pull her pants down far enough to expose a part of her hip. Then I take the scalpel and make a small, shallow incision. And when I do that, Analise screams bloody murder. Ignoring the screams, tears, and blood, I say, "Be happy I didn't cut deeper. I'm truly giving you the kid glove treatment." I tear off some paper towels, put them on the dresser, place the scalpel on them. Then I open the vial and say, "This is black powder, like they used in the old days. Back then, soldiers occasionally used it to cauterize wounds. If I were being mean, I'd pack it deep into the tissue so that when it ignites, the explosion would travel inward, which would not be pleasant. Also, it would almost certainly introduce a dangerous level of toxicity into your blood stream."

I dust the powder over her cut. When I light the match it finally dawns on Analise that I'm going to hurt her very badly. She tries to speak.

"Sorry," I say. "You had your chance. You can talk after this. And if you tell the truth, we won't need to open the second vial."

I place the match against the gunpowder and Analise experiences a level of pain she never knew existed. She shrieks, cries, pisses herself, and falls unconscious for thirty seconds. When she regains consciousness, she sobs like a schoolgirl whose heart's been broken for the first time. The look on her face says she can't believe I did that to her.

"What's your name?" I ask.

She grits her teeth and juts her jaw. "Analise Compton," she says.

I smile. "Good for you. I'm impressed. But I *will* get my answers."

I close the first vial, put it back in the case, then lift her tank top to expose her tits. She spits in my face and calls me a degenerate. I tear off a paper towel and wipe my face and she spits on it again. This time, I tear off several paper towels, wad them up and shove them in her mouth. Then I use another one to wipe my face off. As I reach for the second vial, my phone rings. It's Dani Ripper, telling me the young lady in front of me might very well be Analise Compton. I disagree, end the call, and remove the cap from the second vial. "This is a spray," I tell Analise. "And it's going to hurt like a motherfucker."

Analise can see it in my eyes. She knows I'm telling the truth. She tries to speak, but gags. But I know what she said. She wanted to know what I was planning to do to her. So, I respond, "Have you ever seen those birthday candles that keep re-igniting every time you blow them out? This vial contains a highly-flammable chemical that's nearly impossible to extinguish. We typically spray it on testicles and set them on fire. If we can't put the fire out within ten seconds it produces third-degree burns."

I spray the liquid on one of her nipples, light a match, and...she breaks down. I remove the paper towels from her mouth. Through sobs, she finally tells the truth. After she does, I ask why she didn't tell me the first time I asked.

Her answer? She was afraid I'd kill her.

"Are you going to?" she asks.

"Not today."

"Thank you. I'm sorry I spit on you."

"It's okay. I had it coming."

"If you're done torturing me, can you get that chemical off my boob and cover me up?"

I cover her up.

"What about the chemical on my boob?"

"It's okay."

"If it's a chemical, I want it off."

"It's definitely a chemical: two parts hydrogen, one part oxygen, but it dries on its own."

"H2O? *Water?*"

"Yup."

Her look could knock a mongrel off a gut wagon, but at least she doesn't spit. I cut her loose, clean her hip wound, and call Callie.

Chapter 6

"HER NAME'S ELLEN Topic," I say. "A housewife, from Prairieville, Ohio, recently divorced. No kids, former husband works in a paper mill."

"How'd they find her?" Callie asks.

"Someone posted a look-alike photo on Facebook that triggered a reverse image search at Sensory Resources. One of our recruiters located her, hired her, and passed her on to one of General Barry's handlers. This was her first job."

"Did she ever meet the general?"

"No. Her handler called herself Sloane. Obviously, the same Sloane I spoke to on the boot phone."

"The one who booked Charlotte the hooker?"

"Probably. Wait. How'd you know about Charlotte?"

"I called her. She told me all about your little encounter in Georgetown. Want to know how I got her name and number?"

"I'm listening."

"Ellen gave me the numbers of the two hookers you were supposed to call to set up the rescue. Charlotte was one of them."

"Why would she tell *you* the names and not *me*?"

"She thought someone else should know, in case something went wrong."

"And she trusted *you*?"

"What can I say? Something about my demeanor exudes trust. By the way, Charlotte told me you were the worst fuck she ever had."

"Thanks for sharing. Had she known I was recently shot in the chest she might've given me a better review."

"I doubt it. After all, you weren't suffering from a gunshot wound the several times *I* fucked you."

"How about we keep this about Analise?"

"You mean Ellen?"

"No. Analise."

"What about her?"

"I know where she is."

"Ellen told you?"

"Nope. Ellen only knows she was a divorced woman in a hick town being paid $10,000 a month to "become" Analise Compton. They moved her to a different city, rented a house for her, paid her bills and expenses, and told her not to leave the premises or meet other people."

"What about her family?"

"They said she could speak to her parents and sister on the phone, but couldn't see them, discuss her work, or give them her address. They told her they were with Homeland Security, and planned to give her a specific mission that would have a positive impact on the country. In the meantime her job was to follow Analise's daily blog, match her hair and makeup as closely as possible, find out everything she could about her on the Internet, watch her speeches and press conferences, and master her voice, communication skills, and mannerisms. They told her when the mission started, her pay would jump to $25,000 a week, and after it ended, she'd have a job waiting for her at Homeland, if she wanted it."

"At twenty-five grand a week?"

"I didn't ask. I knew it was bullshit."

"What's her sister look like?"

I laugh. "I didn't ask."

"You're slipping, Donovan. Unless..."

"Unless what?"

"You like Hot Topic."

"Who?"

"Ellen. You *want* her."

"That's ridiculous."

"*Is* it? Then what *do* you want?"

"My billion dollars."

"Good luck with *that*!"

"I don't need luck. I have a plan."

"Does it involve hiding a midget in a hotel mattress?"

I take a deep breath before saying, "Hilarious."

"Don't be so sensitive. Does your plan rely on Ellen somehow?"

"No."

"Then it's time to kill her."

"I agree."

"If you don't, I will. What's your plan?"

"I'm going to threaten the general."

"How?"

"By involving the media."

Callie says, "I'll stop interrupting you with questions if you'll tell me the entire plan all at once. Otherwise, this will take up ten pages."

"Pages?"

"What's the plan?"

"Like I said earlier, I know where Analise is. And you do, too, by the way. As does half the country."

Callie says, "Okay, so I have to interrupt you just this once because I have no clue what you're talking about."

"Hawley told the judges Analise was alive, and in Las Vegas."

"She was referring to Ellen."

"You and I *assumed* that, because we thought Ellen was Analise. But Hawley didn't know about Ellen."

"She probably focused on Analise's image, and her mind tuned in to Ellen, who was portraying Analise."

"Are you *listening* to yourself right now? That's *way* too convoluted! Hawley didn't say Analise's *look-alike* was in Vegas. She said *Analise* was."

"Donovan? I hate to break it to you, but Hawley's a six-year-old girl."

"Maybe so, but she's also a fucking *witch*! I *guarantee* you she knows where the president's daughter is. And not just the city, but the exact location."

"You've come a long way in a few short weeks, Donovan. First it was midgets in mattresses. Now you not only believe in witches, you think your daughter's a card-carrying member. Great. So, what's your plan?"

I tell her. Then I call Rose, who lets me know she and Hawley got home safely yesterday. After telling me about how well the questioning went back in LA, she puts Hawley on the phone. After a short discussion about their trip, I tell her I saw her audition video, where she made Geoffrey fly.

She laughs.

I say, "Do you really know where Analise is?"

"Yes, Papa."

"The exact location?"

"Yes, Papa."

When she tells me, I ask, "Is anyone with her?"

"Two men."

"Do they have guns?"

"Guns and rifles and other things."

"If Analise leaves to go somewhere else, will you know?"

"Yes, Papa."

We talk until she gets bored with the conversation and passes me off to Rose, who agrees to let me know when Analise moves to a new location. After hanging up, I call General Barry's private line and find it's been disconnected.

I call the White House, but his staff refuses to put me through. With nowhere left to turn, I call Charlotte the hooker, and tell her I need to speak to General Barry's people about Analise Compton's extraction. To which she replies...

Chapter 7

"I HAVE NO idea what you're talking about."

"You spoke to my friend, Callie Carpenter, yesterday?"

"I did, and we talked about you. But I don't know anything about Analise Compton or the White House Chief of Staff guy."

"Forget it. When can I see you again?"

"You really *want* to?"

"How could I not? I had a great time."

"You *did?*"

"Of course. Didn't you?"

"Of course!"

We set the time and place. Five minutes later—just as I expected—I get a call from Sloane, who says, "I'm afraid Charlotte's not going to be available to meet you tomorrow."

"Sorry to hear that," I say. "How are the president's approval ratings?"

"Through the roof! You haven't been watching the news?"

"Not really."

"You tried to contact the general. We had an agreement about that, and you've been paid in full. What are you up to, Mr. Creed?"

"I haven't *quite* been paid in full. The truth is, I'm a billion dollars shy, thanks to the general stealing the funds from my Swiss account. I understand why he won't talk to me. But since *you* have his ear I want you to give him a message: tell him I know where the real Analise Compton is hiding, and if he doesn't return my billion dollars I'm going to contact the police and the media."

"I'm sure the general will say he has no idea what you're talking about."

"I'm sure you're right. But here's the thing: if I don't get my money back in six hours I'll tell the world that Analise Compton is hiding out in a certain high-rise apartment building in Las Vegas."

"That's not very specific."

"You want specific? How's this: Bushkin Drive, Apartment 2112. Guarded by two heavily-armed private security guards. If I don't get my money, you, Analise, Randy, General Barry, the two security guards, and at least one Secret Service agent will have a lot of explaining to do."

"Where are you? We should meet to talk about this."

"I don't think so."

Sloane pauses a moment. "Very well. I'll be in touch."

"Call me in four hours."

"*Four*? A moment ago, you said six."

"I did. But this is for *your* benefit."

"How so?"

"Here's what'll happen after we hang up: you'll call General Barry. He'll move Analise to another location, and in four hours you'll call me back and tell me to go fuck myself. Except that when you call I'm going to tell you Analise's *new* location, and you'll only have *two* hours to get my money before all hell breaks loose. The general will move her again, but it won't matter, because wherever she goes, I'll know. And when I fail to get my money, the whole world's gonna know."

Sloane laughs. "You know those silly movies where the evil genius gets the drop on the hero, but instead of killing him he comes up with some crazy death plan where he suspends the hero over a shark-filled tank or a pit full of snakes? Then he leaves the scene and the hero escapes? But before that happens, the evil genius couldn't help but gloat and tell the hero all his plans? Well, you just did that."

"What do you mean?"

"You gave yourself away."

When she ends the call, I walk upstairs to check on Ellen. "How's your hip?"

"How do you think? It's an open, festering wound."

"I know it hurts, and I'm sorry for that. But you have to admit, I gave you numerous warnings, and it could have been a lot worse."

"You set me on fire. Not only that, you sexually abused me."

"I did nothing of the sort."

"You exposed my boobs."

"True, but I didn't *touch* them."

"Touching doesn't enter into it. It's still sexual abuse."

"That doesn't seem right."

"It never does, to men."

I use my phone to access the Internet. Then type in the words "sexual abuse" and am surprised to learn the official definition is as all-encompassing as the cosmos. Among a litany of other acts, it includes derogatory name-calling by a spouse, and using items such as baby oil or lubricants without consent. The definition doesn't specifically mention spraying water on a woman's tits, but I'm pretty sure that's part of the package.

"I stand corrected," I tell Ellen. "I'm sorry. I truly didn't intend to sexually abuse you. I was only trying to torture you as effectively as possible."

"And yet you chose my boobs."

"I did."

"Why?"

"Because you're a woman."

"Do you have any idea how sexist that sounds?"

"Not really. I mean, you *are* a woman, and I was seeking a spot on your body that wouldn't be visible to most people. Being aware that women are typically more focused on their breasts than other body parts, I—"

"*Excuse* me? Where are you getting all this information about women and their focus? From *porn*?"

"Occasionally. But mostly from personal experience."

"You're full of shit. You just wanted an excuse to see my tits."

"That was certainly a factor."

"And you *did* see them."

"Yes."

"And that's sexual abuse."

"I agree. Again, I'm sorry."

"And?"

"I'll never look at them again."

"Why *not*? Was there something *wrong* with them?"

I sigh. Hearing Dani enter the house, I leave the room and Ellen's voice follows me down the stairs: "I have great boobs!" she yells.

Chapter 8

DANI'S ON THE sofa, clutching her knees to her chest, crying softly. Her breakup with Sophie's taking a toll. She's been despondent since we arrived. Though she's upset with me, she's being civil. She wipes her cheeks and makes me a sandwich. After eating, I find a deck of cards on the counter and talk her into playing gin rummy with me until Rose calls. By the time I hang up, Dani's lost her mood. For no other reason than to get her talking, I say, "Before I came downstairs, Ellen accused me of sexually assaulting her."

She narrows her eyes. "*Did* you?"

"Yes. But not the way you think. Still, she convinced me there's a lot I need to know about what constitutes sexual assault, abuse, and harassment."

"Why are you bringing this up?"

"I figure you're a walking encyclopedia on the subject." When she says nothing I add, "Is that not true?"

"I'm not sure what you're trying to imply."

"Just that I know you specialize in locating and helping abused kids, so I'm sure you're current with all the laws. You're also a beautiful woman, and I bet men hit on you every day."

She appraises me coolly, through skeptical eyes. "Where are you going with this?"

"I was hoping you could educate me."

"Why?"

"Because I only know about the obvious things. And now I realize there are gray areas."

"Like what?"

"Well, I just found out if you call me a name, that's sexual harassment."

"That's not true. Not necessarily. I think the name has to have a sexual connotation. Why are you grinning?"

"I was at a party once where a woman flashed her boobs at me. Was that sexual assault?"

She shakes her head as if she can't believe any woman would do such a thing. "Absolutely."

"Even though I enjoyed it?"

She frowns. "Doesn't matter. She shouldn't have flashed them at you without your consent."

"So, if I had asked, 'Will you show me your boobs?' it would've been okay?"

"Absolutely not! If you ask a woman to show you her boobs, *you'd* be guilty of sexual harassment, and possibly abuse."

"Fascinating."

"Glad I could clear it up for you," she says, wryly.

We're quiet until I ask, "Does that make sense to you?"

"Of course."

"Then how does anyone ever get to see a woman's boobs without committing or being the victim of sexual harassment?"

"Boobs have to be revealed as the result of a gradual sequence that progresses one step at a time, with mutual consent being asked and given every step of the way."

"Doesn't that kill the passion?"

"Of course. But you were asking about the politically correct way to enjoy sex. What's the matter, have I ruined it for you?"

"Not at all, since I only consort with hookers."

She gives me a sharp look. "You're still *doing* that? While married to *Trudy*?"

"Trudy and I are divorced."

"Since when?"

"A couple months ago."

"No offense, but you don't seem particularly upset."

I shrug. "I believe in moving forward."

Her lip quivers, and a whole new round of tears starts forming in her eyes.

"Aw, shit," I say. "For that one moment I forgot I made you break up with Sophie. But your situation's different. You guys will be fine."

Dani starts crying. "You couldn't be more wrong. She's done with me. When I gave her the news she never threatened me, never begged me to stay. She's furious. Wouldn't even answer when I called to see if she was okay. It's over. You made me lose the best thing that ever happened to me. And for *what*? A botched kidnapping?"

I sigh. "This is too much." I take out my phone, locate a number, send a text.

"What are you doing?"

"Clean yourself up."

"Why?"

"Sophie's coming."

"What?"

"I just sent for her."

"She's coming *here*?"

"Yeah. Fix yourself up."

She sets her jaw. "What's going on?"

"I'm getting you lovebirds back together."

Dani searches my face. "You couldn't possibly get all that accomplished with a ten-second text."

"What can I say? I'm good."

"Full of shit is what you are."

Before we can debate the merits of her argument, the front door opens. It's Sophie.

Dani does a double-take. Then says, "You knew it all *along*?"

Sophie grins.

Dani calls her a bitch and says, "I can't believe you let me go through all that! And YOU!" she says to me with eyes blazing.

"Relax," I say.

"How long has she *known*?"

"I called her moments after I called you."

"Why?"

"I remembered you said Sophie's cabin wasn't very secluded. I was concerned one of the neighbors might see people here and call her. If they did, she might've called the police."

"But you still made me steal the key to her cabin."

"Yes."

"And you made me break up with her, even though you knew it wasn't necessary."

"That's right."

She turns to Sophie. "And you sat there and watched me break up with you even though you knew it was a phony breakup. You acted like you didn't even care, or want me. You just let me suffer. How could you be so *cruel*?"

Sophie says, "I was paying off part of the favor you owed Donovan."

"The favor was stealing the cabin keys, breaking up with you, and babysitting the phony kidnap victim."

They look at me. Sophie says, "Phony *kidnap* victim? You said you needed a place to hide your daughter, and Dani was going to babysit."

I shrug. "If I told you she was babysitting Analise Compton would you have let us use the cabin?"

Sophie frowns. "You *know* I wouldn't. So you lied to Dani, you lied to me, and you somehow managed to kidnap the wrong person?"

"Yeah. But with regard to the kidnapping, when you see Ellen you'll understand how we made that mistake."

Dani says, "She's a perfect match for Analise. Except for the eyes."

I say, "Are you guys gonna hug, or what?"

They look at each other. Dani says, "How'd you get here five minutes after he texted?"

"I've been staying at Toni and Lucille's."

"Two doors down?"

"Yup."

"Since when?"

"I actually got to Gatlinburg before you did."

Sophie closes the distance between them. Dani says, "I should kick your ass."

Sofe says, "I might enjoy that."

Dani looks at me. "You made me sit here and play cards all afternoon whle Sofe was two doors down?"

I point to the master bedroom. "Why don't you ladies go in there and talk about how awful I am?"

"You don't need me for anything?"

"Not at the moment."

They enter the master bedroom quickly, and close the door.

I go back upstairs, change Ellen's bandage, and say, "Analise's kids weren't in on it, were they?"

"Not to my knowledge."

"So, she was at the ski resort, and somehow the two of you switched places."

"That's right."

"Where and when?"

"There's a cleaning closet in the ladies' bathroom at the ski shop. I was locked inside."

"Who had the key, Analise?"

"There wasn't one. I brought a portable lock with me that fits in the door jamb and lets me lock the door from the inside."

"How'd you get in the closet without people seeing you and thinking you were Analise?"

"I was wearing a hijab."

"So, you were already in the bathroom, then Analise came in, and you changed places with her, and then Callie came in?"

"That's right."

"So how did Analise escape?"

"She had a similar hijab in her purse. She put it on and left before anyone figured out what happened."

"The Secret Service agent guarding Analise at the ski shop."

"What about him?"

"He was in on it, right?"

"I don't know. Probably."

My phone interrupts us. According to my caller ID, it's Sloane. When I answer she says, "As you predicted, and with great joy, I'm ready to tell you to go fuck yourself."

Ignoring her sexual abuse, I say, "I would if I could, since it'd save me a fortune in hookers. But your celebration's a bit premature, since I happen to know where Analise is."

"You're bluffing. You obviously got your information from the guards, but that's no longer an issue."

"Because they're dead."

"I didn't say that."

"No, you didn't. I'm telling *you* they're dead. In case you didn't know."

"Are you saying you've got someone on the inside?"

"I'm only saying I know where they moved Analise."

"Prove it."

Chapter 9

AFTER I GIVE Sloane the address where Analise is, she goes silent a long time. Finally, she says, "We'll need more time to get your money."

"You *had* more time, and chose to waste it. You've now got two hours to wire one billion dollars to my Swedish account."

"The amount confiscated was less than that."

"What *was* the exact amount?"

"Nine hundred eighty-six million and change."

"That'll do."

She says, "I'll give him the message."

Twenty minutes later, she calls back to say: "We can do eight hundred and eighty-four million."

"What happened to the rest?"

"It was donated to the president's election campaign."

"Are you telling me he donated over a hundred million dollars to get the president elected?"

"The president and some assorted Senators and Congressmen. Eight-eighty-four is still a lot of money."

She's right: it is.

Funny thing: a few months ago, I had a billion dollars. One day later, I had nothing. Now, in less than two hours, I'll have $884,000,000. Which means I've suffered a net loss of more than a hundred million. But it doesn't feel like a loss, it feels like a gain. A *huge* gain. So, I tell her: "Wire the money."

Sloane says, "I'll need you to agree to our terms."

"You're in no position to make demands. Nevertheless, I'm willing to hear them."

"There are three: first, you can't directly or indirectly interfere with our plans for Analise Compton. That includes no police, no press, and it also means you can't have someone else interfere on your behalf."

"I'll agree to that."

"Second, you can never disclose any details of the incident to anyone, under any circumstance."

"Agreed."

And third, you have to agree not to kill anyone associated with the incident, or the presidency. That includes all the players, their family members, all government officials, General Barry, and...me."

"Sorry. I can't agree to that. Barry stole a billion dollars from me."

"Are we talking about the same billion you stole from the international crime consortium?"

"We are. And I fully expect the crime consortium to continue trying to kill me. Which is why General Barry should expect no less from me."

She says, "Will you at least agree not to kill *me*?"

Though she can't see it over the phone, I smile. "Sloane?"

"Yes?"

"I like your style."

"Thank you."

I say, "You may know that Ellen Topic gave me two phone numbers I could call to orchestrate her release. Obviously, that was a phony gesture by the general, meant to reassure her. But the phone numbers were real. Callie called them yesterday. One was Charlotte's, and the second was the one you're currently using. Your number also happens to match the one I called from the phone I found at Smith Mountain Lake: the one that was wrapped in a boot."

"Are you asking if I'm the other hooker?"

"Let's just say I don't think it's a coincidence how quickly you called me after I spoke to Charlotte today. So yeah, I think you and Charlotte are not just friends, but co-workers. But you're also General Barry's confidante, the one person in the world he seems to trust. But you're so much more."

"Do tell."

"You're also his facilitator."

"You're giving me far too much credit."

"I don't think so. It's quite impressive."

"For a hooker?"

"For anyone. But it also means you can't be trusted."

"I *can* be, if you agree not to kill me."

"Prove it."

"How?"

"Give me your real name and address."

She tells me her name is Carol Worthington, and gives me an address. I ask if she's married. She's not. I ask if she lives alone. She does. I enter all this information into my phone and say, "If this checks out, you'll have nothing to fear from me."

"It'll check out."

"Good. Expect a personal visit."

"When?"

"When you least expect it."

She hesitates. "What type of visit?"

"A professional one."

"*Your* profession? Or mine?"

"Yours."

"I'm not as pretty as Charlotte," she says.

"Neither am I."

She laughs. "I'll look forward to your visit."

"Me too."

Chapter 10

TO MY SURPRISE, the money shows up in my account within minutes. But the obvious problem remains: if the general stole it the first time, what prevents him from stealing it again? The only person I know with years of experience dealing with Swiss banking is Callie Carpenter, so I descend the steps, sit in Sophie's den, and call her.

"How much are we talking about?"

"Eight hundred and eighty-four million dollars."

"And you want to get the entire amount out of Switzerland today?"

"No. Just out of my current account."

"No problem. I'll give you my guy's name and number and he'll set up an account for you." She pauses. "You know where you made your mistake, right?"

"Trusting the Swiss banking system?"

"No. You kept all your money in the same account. Every client that wired payments to that account knew your account number. That made you vulnerable. You need one account to get the payments, but you need to transfer those funds to several other accounts as soon as they're received. Then you need to clean that money, and get it working for you all over the world."

"I transferred twenty million a year to a domestic account."

"Was it enough?"

"It was till Trudy left."

"You should have set up a number of corporate entities to launder the money."

"I've laundered money before. It didn't go so well."

"You're talking about the plastic surgery center in Vegas. The one that got blown up."

"Yeah. That experience burned me out on money-laundering. But I suppose I could give it another go."

"You can't launder more than eight hundred million on your own. It's a slow and painful process that's better left to professionals."

"*You* did it on your own."

"Not really."

"What about your condo project?"

"That was only forty-million, and it occupied two years of my life and was a total nightmare. It would have taken me twenty years to launder my billion, and I would have made a ton of mistakes."

"So, you hired someone? A professional money-launderer?"

"Yeah. His name's Magnus. But he doesn't do it all himself. He's got six full-time legal experts working on my account."

"You trust them?"

"Of *course* not. But they *fear* me, which is the best incentive not to cheat." She laughs. "If we give them *your* account they won't be able to sleep at night."

"You think they'll accept my business?"

"Of course. They're *attorneys*, after all." She laughs again. "I can't wait till you meet Magnus. He's literally the world's biggest sleaze."

"Worse than Sal Bonadello?"

"Let me put it this way," Callie says. "When Satan needs a great deal on a used car, he calls Magnus."

"If he's so sleazy, why do you use him?"

"He gets the job done."

"What does he charge?"

"Thirty percent."

"*What*? That's *insane*!"

"It's the going rate. If you pay any less, you'll probably lose it all and wind up in jail. But it's not as bad as it sounds. Some of the investments actually turn a profit."

"He's *made* you money?"

"I've probably broken even."

"That'll work. When can I meet this guy?"

"Next week. In the meantime, my banker can help you open some numbered accounts where you can transfer this new money."

"Sounds good. Thanks."

"My pleasure. So. What about Ellen?"

I sigh. "I know you want me to kill her, but—"

"Donovan? She's a loose end. We agreed to keep her alive till you got your money, and we did. If you want to bang her first, go ahead. But she needs to die."

"I know."

I walk back up the stairs and enter Ellen's room. She takes one look at my face and says, "You're going to kill me."

"Yes."

"You said you wouldn't do it today."

"I know."

"But you are?"

"Yes."

"*Why*?"

"You're a loose end."

She does that thing they all do when they know it's time: she cries, pleads, promises not to tell anyone...you know the routine. And when I take a step toward her she says the same thing they all say: "I'll do anything you want. *Anything*! Just don't kill me."

I pause, fascinated as always. "When you say you'll do *anything*, what do you mean by that?"

"Anything. Just tell me what you want. Sex? Money?"

"Would you consider killing yourself?"

"*What?*"

"You said you'd do anything, and the only thing I really need is for you to die. Would you consider killing yourself?"

For a moment, she says nothing. Then she comes at me with a knife.

Chapter 11

CALLIE'S RIGHT: I suck at kidnapping. Before I put Ellen in Sophie's guest room, I checked the bedroom drawers, bathroom drawers and cabinet, checked the closet...but I didn't check the bathroom cubbies, where Sophie keeps her guest towels. The problem's obvious: if this were a stranger's cabin, I would have checked every square inch. But I know Sophie, and it never crossed my mind she might keep a hunting knife under a stack of folded hand towels in the guest bathroom.

But clearly, she did.

Thankfully, Ellen screamed as she charged, which gave me time to think about how Callie would handle the situation. Obviously, a kick is called for. Callie's so fast and accurate with her kicks she could easily launch a front kick and knock the knife right out of Ellen's hand. In my younger days, I could've done the same, and am tempted to try it now, just to see if I still can. But how embarrassed will I be if she slashes my leg? And if she happens to sever my anterior tibial artery, I could die. But even if she nicks it I'll have a difficult time trying to fend her off.

I know what you're thinking: that the arteries to worry about are the ones in my head, chest, abdomen, and pelvis, which are so large that the only place people can stop the bleeding by applying pressure is in Hollywood. It's possible a cut ankle artery wouldn't prevent me from killing Ellen, but why take a chance?

My best bet's a side kick to her stomach. Easy to land, since my leg's a lot longer than her arm. A solid kick will send her flying backwards across the room until the back of her head connects with something solid. Even if she doesn't go down, the kick would knock the breath out of her, disorient her, and almost certainly cause her to drop the knife. Unfortunately, at the precise moment I launch my kick, she trips and falls face-first into my foot, and the impact breaks her neck. If you saw this in a movie you'd swear it was my intent. And that's how I'll portray it to Callie.

Actually, scratch that. Callie would ask me the same question I'd ask her: why would Ellen lower her head while coming at me with a knife? Since I can't come up with an answer, I go ahead and check Ellen's pulse, hoist her over my shoulder, and start heading to the stairs. Then I freeze, remembering her ankle bracelet.

Shit!

I back up, fish my phone from my pocket, locate the app, and disarm the bomb. Then I go down the steps, trusting that Dani and Sophie are still too preoccupied in the master bedroom to worry about what I might be doing. After setting Ellen on the floor, I retrieve the trunk, put her in it, and transport her to the back of the van. Then I gather the clothes Callie gave her, and the personal items, put them in the bag Callie provided, then wipe Ellen's prints from all the areas she may have touched. When all that's done, I walk to the master bedroom and knock on the door.

Both women scream.

Dani yells, "Don't you *dare* come in here!"

I tell her, "I just wanted to let you know I'm taking Ellen for a short drive."

"Not yet!" Dani says. "Sofe wants to meet her."

"Very well," I say. "I'll leave her in her room. But I'm going to grab some fresh air."

"Okay. See you when you get back."

I get in the van and drive all the way to Cincinnati, where I meet Sal Bonadello's associate, John Vanic, who owns Vanic Funeral Home, which has a crematorium in its basement. I wish you could see the look on John's face as he helps me lift Ellen Topic onto his steel table.

"Are you okay?" I ask.

He nods, but there are tears in his eyes.

"You sure you're okay?"

"Yeah, sure," he says, wiping his eyes. "It's just...I voted for the guy."

"This isn't who you think it is."

"Yeah, sure. Of course."

He looks at the trunk. "We can use that instead of our normal container."

"Good to know. Let's do it." I reach for her shoulders, but he says, "Hang on. I gotta ask a couple questions."

"Trust me, you don't want to know."

He says, "Not those types of questions. I need to know if she has a pacemaker, artificial prosthetics, or other types of metal in her body, like titanium."

"Not that I'm aware of. Why's that important?"

"The metal won't melt, and pacemakers can explode."

"She's pretty young. I think we're safe."

"She didn't have cancer, far as you know?"

"Why do you ask?"

"Sometimes bodies contain radioactive cancer seeds or isotopes that were implanted or injected. They have a low boiling point. If she's got those, we need to remove them for the safety of our workers."

"Again, I think we're safe."

He looks at her chest. "What about breast implants?"

"That would be a yes."

"Saline or silicone?"

"I don't know. Why does *that* matter?"

"Silicone melts into a gooey mess. I'd rather not have to scrape it from my equipment if I don't have to."

"What's the alternative?"

"Cut them out before cremation." He looks at her chest again. Then says, "May I?"

I nod.

He exposes her breasts and manhandles them far beyond the definition of sexual assault. Then he says, "Saline. We're good."

We put her back in the trunk and place it on a rack of rolling pins. John preheats the incinerator to 1,100 degrees, then opens the doors, and the trunk slides into the primary cremating chamber, which John calls a retort. When the doors close, a column of flame engulfs the trunk. The gauge shows the temperature's hit approximately 1,800 degrees.

"How long's this going to take?" I ask, expecting him to say ten minutes.

"Two to three hours."

"What? *Seriously?*"

He nods.

"I had no idea."

"You want a sandwich?" he says.

Chapter 12

I DECLINE THE sandwich, but keep a close eye on John the entire 135 minutes it takes to complete the job. Afterward, he asks if I want the ashes.

"Can you get DNA from them?"

"No."

"Then, no. But thanks for asking."

Eight hours later I'm in Washington, DC, making my initial drive-by of Carol Worthington's residence, which turns out to be a condo on the ninth floor of an old, but stately former hotel located a quarter-mile from Dupont Circle. I drive to the back of the building and note that all the parking spaces are occupied, as are the legal spaces on the street as far as the eyes can see. Assuming one parking space per resident, it's clear there are 60-plus residences in the building, and scant parking, which tells me it'd be a waste of time to stake out the premises hoping to catch Carol Worthington, a.k.a. Sloane the Hooker. After twenty minutes of searching, I finally locate a parking spot two city blocks from Carol's building, and feel fortunate to get it. Now, standing in front of the building, I walk up the concrete steps and try the door.

It's locked.

The sign says to press the buzzer. I do, and a voice asks who I'm there to see. I say, "The manager." After thirty seconds, the door lock clicks. I turn the knob, pull the door open, and am greeted by an attractive thirtyish lady who introduces herself as Hadlee Hartsell.

Hadlee says, "We don't have a manager, *per se*, but we *do* offer 24-hour concierge services." She performs a mock curtsey, "That's me. We also provide 24-hour security and maintenance."

"The association fees must be through the roof."

"Believe it or not, they're only three-eighty per month."

"Not bad."

"How can I help you?"

I ask if they have any condos for sale, and she leads me to her office and hands me a small brochure. "The initial units were fully subscribed years ago," she says, "but our units are single-bedroom only, which means there's a strong re-sale market as our owners outgrow their spaces. How did you become aware of our property?"

I tell her the building caught my eye.

Hadlee nods in agreement. "It's a lovely building."

She tells me about the three units currently available (the cheapest of which is $400,000). I tell her that seems high for a one-bedroom unit, but she says, "Actually, it's a bargain. I not only work here, I own a unit on the third floor. They're small, but welcoming, with exposed brick walls, wood floors, recessed lights, granite countertops, and more storage than you'd think. And of course we're ideally located between Dupont and Logan, just steps away from restaurants, groceries, and the Metro."

I laugh. "*Steps* away from the Metro? How many steps, exactly?"

She smiles. "Okay, you caught me. Metro's about two blocks. But everything else is really close. Do you have time to see the main selling feature?"

"As it happens, I do."

"Excellent!"

Hadlee escorts me to the elevator and we ride it all the way to the rooftop, where she shows me the outstanding common area they've created for owners and their guests.

"One of the best views in the entire city," she says, proudly. "We have amazing parties once a month."

"Do you personally organize them?"

"I do."

"When's the next one?"

"Three weeks. But the bar's open every weekend, and when the weather's nice, this is the hottest nightspot in the area."

"Is it open to the public?"

"Only when accompanied by owners, with a limit of four per visit. But I'll write you a guest pass for Friday night, if you'd like to check it out."

"That'd be great. Will you be here?"

She smiles. "Sadly, no."

I smile back. "That breaks my heart."

"Uh huh."

We take the elevator back to the lobby, and I follow her into her office. As she writes the invitation she asks, "Are there any additional questions I can answer for you?"

"Yes. What time do you get off today?"

"Excuse me?"

"I'd like to see you tonight."

Her look says she's deeply offended. But it changes to shock when I say, "I can see why the general trusts you: you're truly special." When she fails to respond, I add, "You're an irresistible combination: charming, bright...adorable. You claimed you weren't as pretty as Charlotte, but I think you're selling yourself short. If given the choice, I'd pick you, every time."

She stares at me a long moment before saying, "What gave me away?"

"When I pressed the button out front you answered it immediately. But there was a thirty-second delay before you clicked the door open."

"So?"

"It seemed like the right amount of time to recognize my face on the outside camera and make some adjustments."

"Like what?"

"When we entered your office, I noticed there was no Hadlee Hartsell nameplate on your desk. But there *is* a nameplate on your credenza that's been turned face down. I'm guessing it says Carol Worthington. I suspect you also turned off your private phone and put it in your handbag, since I dialed it on the rooftop and it gave me an instant busy. I'm sure the general pays you quite well to have that phone on and with you at all times, so the only reason I can imagine it being turned off is because you were with me. It would have been embarrassing if I called to speak to Carol, who lives in the building, and the phone in your purse rang."

"Anything else?"

"Yes. While I'm sure you do quite well in your evening business, purchasing a condo in a building like this requires more than cash and credit. It requires current employment and an extensive work history. I couldn't help but think this would be the perfect job for you."

"Why?"

"I imagine the single-bedroom units are predominantly owned by successful businessmen who commute to work and want a place to stay several nights a week."

"Are you suggesting they're my customers?"

"I am. And I'm willing to bet ten thousand dollars that General Barry owns one of the units."

Carol says nothing.

I say, "The address you gave me was for a ninth-floor unit. Were you lying?"

"No. My unit's on the ninth floor."

"Do you also own one on the third floor, like you claimed?"

"No."

"Where's the general's unit located?"

She looks down at her desk. "Third floor."

She writes something on a sticky note and turns it toward me. The note says: *Please don't kill him in the building*. Then she tears it up and looks in my eyes.

"I won't."

When she continues to stare, I add, "I promise."

"Thank you."

"My pleasure. Can I see you after work?"

She takes a deep breath. "Yes, but not here."

PART 8

Creed & Carol

Chapter 1

AFTER LEAVING CAROL, I book a room in a nearby hotel under an assumed name and sleep for the rest of the afternoon.

After waking up, I fight the urge to order room service. Starved I may be, but since I haven't worked out in days I don my running togs and hit the streets.

Now, back in the room, I order room service, turn on the TV, and learn what the rest of the country already knows: shortly after dawn, someone called a small-town newspaper in Alabama and left a message on their voicemail. The message was given by Analise Compton herself, and she sounded like she was reading from a prepared speech. The recording was turned over to the FBI approximately six hours ago, and after subjecting it to a thorough analysis, its been made public, since that was one of the demands.

Analise said:

"I was kidnapped nearly three days ago and want my family and friends to know I'm alive, in good health. Although I received some minor injuries during the capture, I have been treated with respect. I've been told I'll be

released within seven days after the kidnappers' demands have been met. Their demands are as follows:

One, this recording must be played on national TV before 8:00 p.m. tonight, Eastern Standard Time.

Two, the kidnappers demand twenty million dollars in small, non-traceable United States currency.

And three, the kidnappers want the public to know that the United States currently maintains nearly 800 foreign military bases in more than 70 countries and territories. By comparison, Russia, France, and Great Britain, have approximately 30 foreign bases combined. For this reason, the kidnappers demand the immediate closure of 20% of our nation's foreign bases. They say the U.S. military can decide which ones to close.

Finally, my kidnappers are willing to offer proof of life as follows: they will allow my father to ask a single question of his choice during his next press conference and I will answer it via recorded message within twenty-four hours."

The TV news host says, "Three unnamed White House sources agree the voice on the recording is Analise's, and the FBI announced earlier today they're treating the recording as authentic. The president is expected to give a live statement within the hour."

I text Carol the name of my hotel, and she responds she'll be here at eight forty-five.

I finish my dinner, go for a short walk, get cleaned up, and watch TV while waiting for Carol to arrive. In case you're wondering, the president's statement was short:

"I sincerely hope for their sakes that the kidnappers are indeed treating my daughter with respect. She's a wonderful young lady, daughter, wife, mother, and good friend to all who know her, and as you all know she's been a tireless crusader for women's rights for many years. As a father, I'm

deeply saddened by this situation and gravely concerned for Analise's safety. Nevertheless, the United States of America does not, cannot, and will not negotiate with terrorists. For this reason, I can only appeal to your decency as human beings: please look within your hearts and realize that forcibly removing an innocent person from her family and threatening her life is not a proper way to enrich yourselves or make a political statement. Therefore, I'm asking for the immediate safe return of my daughter to her family. In the meantime, I've been told I can ask one question, and Analise will answer it within twenty-four hours. My question is this: Analise, who kidnapped you?"

I laugh out loud. What a great question!

Chapter 2

"BEFORE WE GET started," Carol says, "I have a few things to say. First, I want to make a plea for Henry's life."

I chuckle. "You call him Henry?"

"What do *you* call him?"

"General, unless we're drinking. Then I call him Hank."

"Very well. I want you to consider sparing Hank's life."

"What else did you want to say?"

"I want to address something you said earlier today."

"Please do."

"You assumed I'm fucking the men who own condos in my building. For your information, that's something I would never do. It's unprofessional, unethical, and would be a violation of my employment contract."

"I stand corrected. And chastened. I'm sorry."

"Your assumption about me was not only rude, but terribly insulting. It upset me all afternoon. Normally I'd keep my mouth shut and hope not to be killed, but your comments were extremely hurtful, and have proven impossible to ignore."

"Please accept my apology. You're right: it was rude and unfair. I won't try to defend my comments. I was wrong to say that, and I'm sorry."

She studies my face. "Thank you. What about Henry?"

"Before I address that, you said you had several things to say. Was there anything else?"

"Yes. I want your promise not to harm me, or allow any harm to come to me."

"You're asking for my *protection*?"

"No. I just mean I want you to promise not to kill me or direct any of your associates to kill me."

I nod. "I won't let any of my associates harm you in any way, and I'll personally make every effort to be your close and trusted friend."

"That's not quite what I asked," she says, "but it's progress. Thank you."

"You're welcome. Is that everything?"

"Yes. Except I want you to know that although Charlotte and I are close friends, I've been out of the business for several years. I only see Henry."

"And yet you're here."

"Yes."

"Can I ask why?"

"I'm fighting for my life."

"And what else?"

"I'm hoping you'll spare Henry. But if you don't, I'm hoping you'll value my friendship and affection enough to keep me alive."

"You're being practical."

"Exactly. And if you were honest with your compliments today, I'm sure you can find a way to utilize my talents."

"Assuming I can trust you."

"Assuming that," she agrees. "And not that you know me, but I'm an extremely loyal person. Which is why I'm pleading for Henry's life."

I nod. "Here's my problem with Hank: he not only *stole* my money, he emptied my entire account."

She frowns. "Did *you* leave anything behind when you stole the billion dollars from the crime syndicate?"

"As a matter of fact, I did."

She looks surprised. "How much?"

"A hundred million."

She arches both eyebrows. "*Why?*"

"Because it's the right thing to do."

Carol cocks her head to see if I'm kidding. When she realizes I'm not, she says, "I'm sure Henry wasn't aware there's a protocol among thieves. But on the plus side you have eight hundred and eighty-four million dollars, which is far more than you left the criminals."

I nod. "I've been thinking about that unusual sum of money."

"What do you mean?"

"I find it hard to believe the general made $102,000,000 in campaign donations. I'm thinking he might have donated *two* million, and kept the hundred million for himself."

"I can assure you he did not."

"Okay, go ahead."

"Excuse me?"

"Assure me. How do you know he didn't?"

"Because...and I'm being 100% honest here...he gave me part of it."

"How big a part?"

"Six million."

"Be honest: how much did he contribute to the campaigns?"

"I don't know. Bear in mind, Henry never said how much he stole or who he stole it from. *You're* the one who provided that information.

So, when he said he still had $884,000,000, I was shocked. But I remember him saying that the president couldn't have been elected without him because he raised forty-six million for his campaign."

"That number has the ring of truth. It also tells me Hank kept fifty million for himself."

She bites her lip. "Is that a number you can let slide?"

"No. Sorry."

"If he returns the fifty million, will you spare his life?"

"No."

She pauses, then says, "I spent approximately a million dollars paying off my condo, car, student loan, and helping my parents. But I still have about five million I can return to you."

"Please: I want you to keep it."

"Seriously?"

"Yes. It's part of the protocol. Among—I believe you said—*thieves*."

"I—"

I laugh. "It's okay. I wasn't offended."

"Not to complain, but...can you explain your thought process?"

"There are no *written* rules, of course, but there *is* a certain honor among thieves at this level. As I said earlier, it's extremely poor form to clean someone out completely."

"How much should you leave?"

"At least 10%."

"Like I said, I'm sure Henry didn't know."

I smile. "Sorry to burst your bubble, but he's the one who taught me that. He cleaned me out hoping I wouldn't suspect him. And it nearly worked."

"What made you suspect him?"

"He offered me a kidnapping job."

"So?"

"I don't do kidnapping. But somehow, he knew I'd take it. Because I needed the money."

After a short pause she says, "Tell me the rest of the protocol, and how it means you don't expect me to repay you."

"Hank stole the money, not you. How he spent it is immaterial. He donated some to the campaign, gave some to you, probably paid off some of his own bills. Doesn't matter. The six million you got was a gift from Hank. He's already on the hook for it."

"But you could easily recover the money I still have."

"Yes, and I expect most people in my situation would force you to return it. But you've been 100% honest with me, and I know this will sound premature, but...there's something about you that inspires trust. I'd like to explore a relationship."

She shows me a curious look. "What type?"

"Long term. I'm confident there are lots of ways we can help each other."

"So, a business relationship."

"Yes. In the sense you'll be well-compensated for your services."

"Including sexual services?"

"In a perfect world, yes. But I'm aware you may not feel the same way about me, since I'm the one who's going to end your current relationship."

"You're giving me a choice?"

"Of course."

"You do understand I came here tonight assuming we'd have sex."

"I hoped so, but it won't be fun if you aren't interested."

"Just to clarify: you're letting me live, you're letting me keep the money, and I don't have to fuck you."

"That's correct."

She smiles. "In that case, I'm all yours."

Chapter 3

WITH THE BROAD shoulders of a swimmer, Carol's upper torso is well-toned, and features smallish breasts with nipples tauter than a mountain climber's rope. Her abdomen is well-exercised, and tapers perfectly into the kind of hips that'll draw you in faster than a carnival barker at a state fair. Her scent is alluring, natural, and reminiscent of vanilla, almond, and black pepper. Her panties are sexy, not showy, and I remove them with all the reverence and care I'd exercise when unwrapping a priceless gift. For this, she rewards me with...

Well, you get the picture: Carol was amazing.

Was it the best sexual experience of my life?

Yeah, probably.

What made it so special?

She blended the enthusiasm of a college girl with the experience of a seasoned hooker. Not only that, but she was relatively quiet in her lovemaking, a plus for me, since most hookers are such shameless over-actors they'd make Al Pacino blush. Afterward, she was attentive without being clingy, displaying a sincere interest in lying beside me and chatting. I asked if she heard what the president asked Analise during his press conference. She had not, and when I told her she howled with laugher. Then she said, "While we're on the subject, can I ask you something?"

"Please do."

"After Henry's people moved Analise, how did you know where she went?"

"I can't tell you. And even if I *could*, you'd never believe me."

She makes a pouty face. "Now I *have* to know!"

"Sorry."

"Henry used the top people in the country to move her. They were extremely careful."

"I'm sure they were."

"You're really not going to say how you knew?"

"Nope."

She giggles. "It's okay, I'm just messing with you. But you certainly taught me *one* thing: if I ever do something wrong, there's no place I can hide."

I frown. "That sounds *terrible*. I don't want you to *fear* me."

"Too late!" she says, smiling.

My phone vibrates on the nightstand. When I check the message, my heart sinks. "Aw, shit."

"What's wrong?" Carol says.

I sigh, put the phone back on the nightstand.

Carol says, "You seem so *sad*. What happened, just now?"

"I trusted you."

She starts to say something, but I've already got her by the throat. As she flails her arms and kicks her legs helplessly I tell her how I stationed Callie Carpenter in the stairwell two hours ago, and how she just reported killing the two men General Barry sent to kill me.

When Carol's as dead as she's going to get, I text Callie to join me.

"Pretty lady," she says. "Good lay?"

"Not in your league."

"You're lying through your teeth. But thanks for making the effort."

"Thank *you*, for being here for me. What happened to the hitmen?"

"They're in the stairwell. We should probably leave. Oh, and by the way, you're naked."

"Am I?"

I'd forgotten.

While I gather my clothes and personal items, Callie searches through Carol's handbag. Moments later she triumphantly holds up the wireless voice transmitter and says, "Got it!" Before smashing it, I say, "General? You're next."

Callie says, "You're not planning to kill him anytime *soon*, are you? Because you *know* he's gonna be extra careful."

"I'm not even going to kill him this *year*," I say. "But I like the idea of making him sweat." I pause. "What were they waiting for?"

"The hitmen?"

"Yeah."

"What's the last thing you said before I sent the text?"

"She wondered how I knew where they moved Analise."

"And you refused to tell her?"

"Yes."

Callie nods. "There you go. This whole evening centered around getting that piece of information. Can I ask *you* something?"

"Sure."

"Why are you still naked?"

I glance at Carol.

Callie says, "You *didn't*."

I shrug.

She walks over to the bed, takes a closer look at Carol's private area and says, "God *damnit*, Donovan!"

Trooper that she is, she helps me carry Carol to the shower, where I hold her legs up and remove all traces of our encounter. Then I finish packing my suitcase, get dressed, and Callie helps me wipe all fingerprints from the scene. As we climb into her rental car she says, "I suppose we need to clean the van."

"We do. Can you follow me?"

"Of course."

After we dump and clean the van I set it on fire and climb into Callie's rental car. She drives us to Dulles International, where we return her car and take the midnight flight to Salt Lake City. When we arrive, we rent a car, drive to the nearest hotel, book two rooms, and sleep till three p.m. Then Callie joins me in my room, where we order some food and do what half the country's doing: tuning in to a news station on TV to wait for Analise's response to her father's question.

At 5:35, it comes.

Analise says,

"I want to thank my captors for continuing to treat me well. In response to my father's question, I'm sorry, but I don't know their names, nor have I seen their faces. I'm being heavily guarded, and have been moved to at least two locations. My captors were kind to allow me to offer this proof of life, but this is the last time I'll be allowed to make a public announcement. My captors have decided to forego their demand for the twenty million dollars, and ask only that the United States shut down twenty percent of their foreign bases. My captors feel this is a small, but significant action that will start a dialogue toward establishing world peace. My captors have assured me that if twenty percent of the foreign bases are closed within sixty days, I will be returned safely to my family. Otherwise, I'll be killed. There will be no further concessions, no further discussions. I love my children, love my husband, my parents, and I love the United States of America."

"Quite moving," Callie says. "You think they'll close the bases?"

"Probably. I'm sure far more than twenty percent of them have outlived their usefulness."

"Why do you suppose they made that a demand?"

"Because it sounds like a big deal that's really a big nothing. Congress has been considering eliminating those bases for years, they've just never put it to a vote. Despite what the president said about refusing to cater to terrorists' demands, I'm sure Congress will overrule him, since doing so will save hundreds of millions of dollars."

"Wouldn't it be hilarious if the general kills her during the extraction?"

I look at poor, sick Callie and say, "Hilarious isn't the first word I'd use."

With dinner behind us, I say, "You still want to do what we came here to do?"

"Absolutely. We owe it to him."

PART 9

Callie & Creed

Chapter 1

WHEN DISABLED IRAQ War veteran Orlando Gonzales jumped the North Fence of the White House at 7:20 pm on Friday, September 19, 2014, he ran straight to the North Portico doors and gained entrance to the White House. Why were the doors unlocked?

I have no idea.

But I *do* know that just outside those doors is an alarm that would've alerted the guards that security had been breached.

If the alarm had been working.

But it was disabled after the White House Usher's Office complained it had been malfunctioning.

I get that. Alarms go bad from time to time. But when they do, we get them repaired, right?

Not the White House.

Instead of reporting the broken alarm, one of the guards cut the power source to keep it from ringing erratically. As a result, he left the entrance vulnerable to attack.

Why am I bringing this up?

Because it's the little things we do that get us killed.

Twenty minutes ago, Callie and I planned to gain entry to a particular home the same way crooked alarm installers do: we were going to spend hours setting off the alarm over and over until the owner, a wealthy divorcee, got angry enough to stop setting it. She'd call the alarm company to report the unit broken, and they'd explain they can't do anything about it tonight, since it's after hours. They'd tell her to call the main number tomorrow to set an appointment to get it serviced.

In the meantime, like the North Portico doors of the White House, the lady's home would be vulnerable to attack.

But we didn't have to do all that because the lady never set the alarm in the first place. So, Callie and I picked the backdoor lock, entered the house, and spent the past two hours snooping through her things.

It's amazing what you can learn about people when entering their home unannounced. For example, we learned by checking the lady's phone messages that her ex-husband died a couple days ago, and her grieving kids are staying with her parents while she focuses on finalizing his funeral arrangements. We assumed she'd be home hours ago, but no. So here we sit, in her den, talking about silly stuff, like we often do in these situations. Usually Callie starts things off, and this time's no different.

"What's the saddest thing you ever saw?" she asks.

"I believe you asked me that years ago. My answer hasn't changed."

"Tell me again."

"When I was a kid, my grandfather took me on a trip out west. We spent the night at a campground, and the next morning I got up and went for a walk. After a while, I came to an old fence, about 50 feet long. On each fencepost, I saw a turtle, fighting for its life."

"I remember," she said. "Some bastard positioned the turtles on the fence posts so that their legs would move, but they couldn't fall off. He was going to boil them to death in the heat, but you saved them."

"Yup."

"And the kid that put them there was older and bigger than you, and he came at you, and you killed him."

I nod.

"That was your first kill, right?"

"Yeah. What about you?"

"My first kill or the saddest thing I ever saw?"

"Saddest thing."

"You remember the businessman I poisoned on the plane just as it was about to land in Louisville?"

"Vaguely. Who hired you?"

"Bennie G. He asked for you, but you were on your honeymoon, so you gave me the job."

"Right. That was the married guy having an affair with Bennie's daughter. What's the sad part?"

"They kept us on the plane for over an hour, and I missed my flight. Then a weather front moved in and they cancelled all the flights till the next day, so I had to spend the night in Louisville."

"What am I missing?"

"As I walked through the baggage claim on my way to get a cab I saw the guy's kid, probably sixteen years old, sitting all alone crying. He just sat there, watching his dad's suitcase go around the conveyor belt over and over, knowing his dad was never coming to get it."

"Why was the kid sitting *there*?"

"They were holding his dad somewhere for the coroner. They probably told the kid to wait in baggage claim until they were ready to release the body."

"Where was the mom?"

"How the fuck would *I* know?"

"I agree that's pretty damn sad. But I've got a question."

"What now?"

"If his dad's suitcase was the only one on the conveyor, why was it still going around over and over for all those hours? Don't they shut it off after a few minutes?"

"Maybe it was stuck, and they didn't know it. The kid was the only one there."

"Why didn't he pull it off the conveyor?"

"You want me to track him down and ask him?"

"Yeah."

"Fuck you!"

I change the subject. "Ever heard of tardigrades?"

She looks at me with sudden interest. "Is that a real thing?"

"It is. I was reading an article about how tardigrades are the toughest animals on the planet."

"Never heard of them. Are they cuddly?"

I laugh. "They're tiny."

"Microscopic?"

"Not that small. They run about one-fiftieth of an inch, and have four pairs of legs. Each leg has four to eight claws that are known as disks."

"How tough are they?" she asks.

"You remember in 2007 when the European Space Agency sent 3,000 animals into orbit?

"No."

"Well, they did, and the tardigrades survived for 12 days *outside* the capsule!"

"Whoa!"

"According to scientists, they're the closest any species comes to immortality. They've survived on Earth more than 100 million years, and some species, thought dead, have been brought back to life after being immersed in water for a few hours."

"How long had they been dead?"

"In one case, a group of tardigrades was taken from the dried moss in a museum exhibit that was more than 100 years old and brought back to life."

Callie ponders it a minute, then says, "I bet I could find a way to kill them."

I laugh. "I bet you could."

We're quiet a few minutes. Then Callie says, "Strangest death."

"We've done this one before, also."

"I know, but it's been a while. And I've got some new ones."

"Okay, I'm game. But for me, nothing beats Sigurd the Mighty, in the year 892."

"Remind me about Sigurd."

"He killed a guy named Mael Brigte and cut his head off and strapped it to his saddle. As he rode his horse, Brigte's head bounced against his leg and caused a fatal infection."

She laughs. "I love that he was killed by the guy *he* killed!"

"Me too. Tell me your new ones."

"The deaths aren't new, it's just that I only read about them recently. You remember the band ELO?"

"Electric Light Orchestra? What about them?"

"One of the members, Mike Edwards, died when a giant bale of hay rolled down a hill and crashed into the van he was driving."

"When was that?"

"2010."

"Weird. What else do you have?"

"You know the whiskey, Jack Daniels?"

"Intimately."

"Well, the actual owner, Jack Daniel, had a safe he couldn't get open one day, and it pissed him off. He kicked it so hard he cut his toe and it got infected, and he died."

"When?"

"1911."

"You hear that?"

"Yeah."

"I think she just pulled into the driveway."

Chapter 2

WHILE CALLIE HIDES behind the granite island in the center of the kitchen, I take the dark side of the door that leads from the garage to the kitchen. "Just like old times," I whisper.

Except it's not.

In the old days, we typically dealt with multiple thieves and murderers, and stood a 50-50 chance of getting killed or seriously injured. Tonight, we're targeting a pampered 38-year-old woman who works for her dad. It takes her forever to come through the door, but when she finally does, I take her down without a sound. Then her giant boyfriend comes through the door yelling, "What the *fuck?*"

That was a surprise!

Callie stands, puts two bullets in his chest, pauses, then shoots him in the head.

"Big guy," she says.

I place the lady on one of her dining room chairs and bind her wrists and ankles with nylon cable ties. When she regains consciousness I say, "Hello, Miriam."

She handles the situation exactly the way you'd expect: fear, shock, horror…that multiple. She asks about her boyfriend.

Callie says, "He's in the garage."

"Is he okay?"

"Yeah. He's unconscious, though."

"Wh-what do you want?"

I say, "We're friends of Ted, your ex-husband."

"Teddy died."

Callie says, "I know. Guess who killed him?"

Miriam's eyes go wide.

I say, "Before he died, Ted told us all about his life, and how you ran off with another guy, a pro basketball player."

"Speaking of which," Callie says, "How come we don't recognize him?"

It takes her a full minute to find her voice. But eventually she says, "He plays semi-pro."

"What's his name?"

"Austin Laskieris."

"Ted said you were bragging about the size of his dick."

Miriam shakes her head.

Callie says, "I checked. It *is* big. But it was rude as hell for you to say that to Ted."

Miriam's having a hard time following the conversation. She's crying, and her head's hurting like hell from when I choked her and interrupted the flow of oxygen to her brain. But mostly she's feeling the effects of not having control for what I suspect is the first time in her life. Again, she asks what we want.

Callie says, "You ruined Ted's *life*. Turned his *kids* against him. Your father *fired* him. He was driving for *Uber*, living with his fucking *parents*!"

Miriam suddenly finds her backbone. "I'm sorry, but didn't you just tell me you *killed* him?"

"*You* killed him," Callie says. "We only put him out of his misery. Were you planning to speak at his funeral? Say nice things about him?"

"Yes, of course. He's the father of my children."

Callie shakes her head in disgust. "Ted deserves better."

Miriam narrows her eyes. "If you think so, maybe *you* should speak at his funeral."

"Maybe I *will!*" Callie says. She points at me and says, "He and I hardly ever like people. But we both liked Ted."

"How nice. And how long had you known him before breaking his neck?"

"About twenty minutes," I say.

Miriam nods. "That's Teddy, all right. Whining, sniveling, crying about his terrible life. Poor Teddy, always the victim. The truth is, he was a loser."

Callie says, "Is that part of your eulogy?"

Miriam screams Austin's name, then looks at me with great concern.

"He's fine," I say. "Just unconscious."

"For how long?"

"Hours. We gave him a sedative. What's wrong?"

"He has to undergo routine blood tests. If they find an illegal substance they could fire him."

I point at Callie and say, "At the moment, I think you've got bigger issues to worry about."

Chapter 3

CALLIE SAYS, "DID you know my partner can tell fortunes?"

Miriam says nothing.

Callie says, "He doesn't read palms. He reads tits."

Miriam and I have no clue where this is going, but she's a lot more concerned about it than I am.

"That's disgusting," she says.

For no other reason than to play along, I wink at Callie and say, "I admit reading tits is an underappreciated talent."

"One that only works with *women*, I'm sure," Miriam says, with a huff.

"Not necessarily," I say. "*Any* breast will do. But in my experience, a man's fortune generally follows a woman's breasts."

Callie laughs out loud. Then says, "I'd *love* to know Miriam's future. I assume you'll need to examine both breasts?"

"Nope. One is sufficient."

Callie rips open Miriam's blouse. "Can you tell her fortune if she's wearing a bra?"

I say, "Can a palm reader tell *your* fortune if you're wearing gloves?"

Callie grins, claps her hands with delight, produces her knife, and severs Miriam's bra between the cups. Then she says, "Never mind. Ted was right. There's not much here to see."

As Callie presses her knife to Miriam's throat, Miriam screams for Austin again and again. Callie says, "I told Ted I was gonna cut your nipples off and sew them into your mouth. But I forgot to bring a needle and thread. Do you happen to have a sewing kit?"

Miriam shakes her head no, and starts begging for her life. "What about my *kids*?" she says.

"They're better off without you," Callie says.

"Not true!" Miriam says. "I *love* them! They just lost their father. If you kill me, they'll never recover!"

"That sounds *awful*," Callie says. "Should we go ahead and kill them, too?"

"No!"

"Are you sure?"

Miriam nods her head as vigorously as she can with a razor-sharp knife blade against her throat. "Please," she says. "Just kill me. But don't hurt my kids."

Callie says, "Well...since you said *please*, I'll honor your wishes."

After slitting Miriam's throat Callie says, "Notice how she never peed her pants?"

I hadn't thought about it, and tell her so.

Callie says, "I sort of liked her."

"You like everyone after the fact."

She gives me a look. "You were *great* with that whole breast-reading thing. You took that premise and ran with it!"

"So?"

"So, where's this sudden mood coming from?"

I glance at Miriam's breasts, covered in blood. "We sexually assaulted her."

"You think?"

"We didn't need to expose her tits. We could have just killed her."

Callie frowns, closes the distance between us, shoves her hand down my pants. "Thank God!" she says. "I thought maybe you left your balls back at the hotel in Washington." She pauses. "Where's all this coming from? The bitch you cremated?"

I nod.

Callie says, "You can live that way in your *personal* life, but not on the job."

"Why not?"

"Because rules of consent don't apply. Think about it: do we ask our victims for their consent before *murdering* them? No! And torture *always* involves sexual assault. The minute you choked Miriam out you assaulted her body. When she passed out in your arms you were holding her against her will. That's sexual assault, Donovan. How can we *possibly* torture people effectively if we remove the threat of sexual assault? If I'm torturing you, you have to be 100% convinced I'll sever your dick with a rusty razor, or nail your balls to a stump. If not, how am I ever gonna get you to talk?"

"Good point."

"You know this instinctively. Just last night you had sex with that Carol lady, and I'm sure the sex was consensual."

"It was."

"Then you killed her."

"True, but I strangled her. I didn't assault her sexually."

"Oh no? Because I seem to remember you spreading her legs under the boiling hot water in the shower to remove all traces of semen. You don't consider that sexual assault?"

"Not really."

"Perfect! That proves you can separate your everyday life from your job. Do what you always tell me to do."

"What's that?"

"Don't overthink your job. You wanna be Prince Charming on your own time? Great. No wonder the women love you. But when you're working, those same women need to believe you'd set their tits on fire without batting an eye."

"Thanks for the pep talk. Who was it that said you'd never be a great mom?"

"Me."

Chapter 4

AN HOUR LATER, we're sitting in a sports bar, having a drink, when the Celtics game is interrupted by a news feed that starts with live footage of Analise Compton being rescued and hustled into a van. The view changes to an aerial shot. Callie says, "Is that your estate?"

"Sure as hell looks like it."

Now it's on all the TVs in the bar. The announcers are saying the FBI determined Analise Compton was kidnapped by two people, Donovan Creed and Callie Carpenter, who were holding her at Creed's Virginia estate. We watch in horror as our photos are superimposed over the firefight taking place in the background. Callie and I sneak out of the bar and rush to her car.

"You think Anson's okay?" she says.

"I don't know. I hope so."

"What do you think happened?"

"General Barry launched a preemptive strike."

"They're probably raiding my place, even as we speak."

"I guarantee it."

"Did you get your money transferred?"

"I'm not sure."

She starts the car. "You'd better check."

By the time we've traveled twenty miles, I get my answer: my money's safe.

"That's wonderful," Callie says. "What now?"

I say: "If you could look like anyone in the world, whose face would you choose?"

"Margaret Thatcher's."

"For real?"

"Don't be an ass." She pauses. "Is this your clumsy way of saying we need new faces?"

"Yes. And IDs to match."

"Easy for *you* to say. You've done it before. I happen to *like* my face."

"I like it too."

"Maybe I can get by just changing my hair and makeup."

"Are you being serious?"

She sighs. "God damnit, Donovan! My life was perfect, and now it's shit. And all because you took that fucking kidnapping job."

"I know. I'm sorry."

She pulls over and stops the car. "I'm sorry."

"For what?"

"Saying that just now. You're the only reason I'm still alive. I never would have had a nickel, if not for you. You're the only true friend I've ever had."

I press her hand to my lips and kiss it.

"Sexual assault," she says, grinning. Then she says, "We've got tons of money, we're smart...and we've still got each other. If we can get through the next few weeks, we'll be fine."

"I agree."

Callie says, "If you think about it, it's kind of exciting."

"What is?"

"We're about to become the most wanted people in history! Bigger than Bonnie and Clyde!"

I laugh. "It's okay if things will never be the same. We can make them better."

"If I'm being honest," she says, "I've been bored out of my skull these last few years."

"Really?"

"I swear to God. And you know what else? *Fuck* our old lives! I can't *wait* to see what the next chapter brings."

"Me either. But we'll probably have to, no faster than Locke writes."

She chuckles. "We ought to move in with him."

"Who, John Locke?"

"Why not? He's got a basement *and* an attic. Wouldn't that be hilarious?"

"Could be. You know what else we need? A different car."

"I'll see if I can find us one."

As I sit quietly, watching the city lights streaming past the passenger window, it suddenly hits me. "Holy shit! You might not need a new face after all!"

"What do you mean?"

I press a button on my phone. When Rose answers I say, "Correct me if I'm wrong, but didn't you say you and Hawley can make people invisible?"

Callie looks at me and smiles broadly. "God, I love you!" she says.

THE END

Personal Message from John Locke:

I LOVE WRITING books! But what I love even more is hearing from readers. If you enjoyed this or any of my other books it would mean the world to me if you'd click the link below so you can be on my notification list. That way you can receive updates, contests, prizes, and savings of up to 67% on eBooks immediately after publication!

Just click this link: http://www.DonovanCreed.com, and I'll personally thank you for trying my books.

John Locke

New York Times Best Selling Author

Has received more than 10,000 Five-Star Reviews!

8th Member of the Kindle Million Sales Club

(Members include James Patterson, George R.R. Martin, and Lee Child)

John Locke had 4 of the top 10 eBooks on Amazon/Kindle at the same time, including #1 and #2!

...Had 6 of the top 20 books at the same time!

...Had 8 books in the top 43 at the same time!

...Has written 36 books in seven years in six separate genres,

All best-sellers!

...Has been published throughout the world in numerous languages by the world's most prestigious publishing houses!

...Winner, Second Act Magazine's Story of the Year!

...Named by Time Magazine as one of the "Stars of the DIY-Publishing Era"

Wall Street Journal: "John Locke (is) transforming the 'book' business"

Donovan Creed Series:

Lethal People
Lethal Experiment
Saving Rachel
Now & Then
Wish List
A Girl Like You
Vegas Moon
The Love You Crave
Maybe
Callie's Last Dance
Because We Can!
This Means War!
The President's Daughter

Emmett Love Series:

Follow the Stone
Don't Poke the Bear
Emmett & Gentry
Goodbye, Enorma
Rag Soup
Spider Rain

Dani Ripper Series:

Call Me!
Promise You Won't Tell?
Teacher, Teacher
Don't Tell Presley!
Abbey Rayne
Hot Mess Express!

Dr. Gideon Box Series:

Bad Doctor
Box
Outside the Box
Boxed In!

Other:

Kill Jill
Casting Call
When David Died
Sorority Girl
Daisy & Bobby

Kindle Worlds:

A Kiss for Luck (Kindle Only)

Non-Fiction:

How I sold 1 Million eBooks in 5 Months!

Printed by Amazon Italia Logistica S.r.l.
Torrazza Piemonte (TO), Italy